Christi ... S0-BXV-820
1310 ... Rd. B2
Roseville, MN 55113
651-633-6479 Ext. 3

| DATE DUE | |
|----------|--|
|          |  |
|          |  |
|          |  |
|          |  |
|          |  |
|          |  |
|          |  |
|          |  |
|          |  |
|          |  |
|          |  |

*Books by Calvin Miller*

---

*BURNING BUSHES AND MOON WALKS*

*GUARDIANS OF THE SINGREALE*

*A HUNGER FOR MEANING*

*FRED 'N' ERMA*

*IF THIS BE LOVE*

*THE LEGEND OF BROTHERSTONE*

*ONCE UPON A TREE*

*THE PHILLIPPIAN FRAGMENT*

*POEMS OF PROTEST AND FAITH*

*THE SINGER TRILOGY*

*THE SINGER*

*THE SONG*

*THE FINALE*

*SIXTEEN DAYS ON A CHURCH CALENDAR*

*STAR RIDERS OF REN*

*THE TABLE OF INWARDNESS*

*THE TASTE OF JOY*

*TRANSCENDENTAL HESITATION*

*THE VALIANT PAPERS*

*A VIEW FROM THE FIELDS*

*WAR OF THE MOON RHYMES*

*WHEN THE AARDVARK PARKED ON THE ARK*

# Fred'n'Erma

## Calvin Miller

INTERVARSITY PRESS
DOWNERS GROVE, ILLINOIS 60515

©1986 by Inter-Varsity Christian Fellowship of the United States of America

*All rights reserved. No part of this book may be reproduced in any form without written permission from InterVarsity Press, Downers Grove, Illinois. No performance of this work, in whole or in part, is permitted for any purpose without the prior written consent of InterVarsity Press.*

*This drama is a work of fiction. Names, characters, places and incidents are either the product of the author's imagination or are used fictitiously. Any resemblance to actual persons, living or dead, or to organizations, events or locale is entirely coincidental.*

*InterVarsity Press is the book-publishing division of Inter-Varsity Christian Fellowship, a student movement active on campus at hundreds of universities, colleges and schools of nursing. For information about local and regional activities, write IVCF, 233 Langdon St., Madison, WI 53703.*

*Distributed in Canada through InterVarsity Press, 860 Denison St., Unit 3, Markham, Ontario L3R 4H1, Canada.*

*Cover and interior illustrations: Joe DeVelasco*

*ISBN 0-87784-574-3*

*Printed in the United States of America*

**Library of Congress Cataloging in Publication Data**
*Miller, Calvin*
*Fred 'n' Erma*

*I. Title.    II. Title: Fred and Erma.*
*PS3563.I376F7        1986        812'.54        86-2968*
*ISBN 0-87784-574-3*

| 17 | 16 | 15 | 14 | 13 | 12 | 11 | 10 | 9 | 8 | 7 | 6 | 5 | 4 | 3 | 2 | 1 |
|----|----|----|----|----|----|----|----|---|---|---|---|---|---|---|---|---|
| 99 | 98 | 97 | 96 | 95 | 94 | 93 | 92 | 91 | 90 | 89 | 88 | 87 | 86 | | | |

# Prelude

[A teen-age figure sits at a desk lit by a single, dim study lamp. Before him on the table is an open Bible and a sheet of paper which he scratches at busily. Suddenly he stops, stands abruptly, closes the Bible and turns to the audience.]

MILO MACARTHUR: Hello. . . . Sorry. You surprised me. . . . I was just doing a little Bible study. It's Sunday morning! [Picks up Bible.] Most of my friends have quit reading this book—if they ever started. It's not cool, so I don't tell most of my friends that I read it. But Mom likes me to read it, so I do. She also likes me to go to church, so I do that too. Church sure is hard work. I don't understand what Mom sees in it—but she loves it. So does my little sister! Dad? Well, there's no use going into all of this since you'll find out all about it soon enough anyway.

The play you are about to see is just plain typical. It's about the church we go to—Tranquility Community Church. There are lots of troubles in this church . . . my church! Actually, I guess it's God's church. And most of the time God is welcome to it.

Folks sure make a lot of trouble. In fact, trouble here is as regular as the offering plate.

Oh, by the way, I'm Milo MacArthur. I may not say much as this play goes along. But I hope you'll take time to listen and watch. The pastor is named Smith: he does a lot of talking about joy and peace, but to be honest with you, nobody much is happy here right now. We all agree that love is the way of the Christian life. We all agree . . . that is, till it gets down to church business. Then I'm afraid it gets to be every man for himself—or every woman.

Last year we weren't too happy around here because we adopted a new constitution. The year before that, thirty families quit the church over . . . uh . . . uh . . . oh, well, I can't remember, but this year it's . . . well, you'll find out about that soon enough too.

You want to meet my family? Here they are! [Lights slowly come up on three people sitting in chairs arranged like automobile seats.] Here's my dad, Fred—my mom, Erma—and my sweet, little, pesty sister, Dawn Marie. Right now I better just get in the back seat so I can get to this happy, little church when they do. If I don't, who knows what Dad will say. He thinks I'm a loud-mouthed teen-ager. All I know is that I didn't start this quarrel he thinks I have with life—but I hate losing so I just keep talking. I like getting the last word.

Well, it's Sunday. Here goes nothing! [Milo slips into the back seat.]

# ACT I

# Scene I

## Always on Sunday

[Erma is irritated as the car jiggles along while she attempts to read her Bible study guide.]

ERMA: Really, Fred . . .

FRED: Erma, if you wanna drive, be my guest!

ERMA: You're sure a grouch this morning, Fred!

FRED: I am *not* a grouch! It's just that I don't like this brown suit. How many times do I have to tell you, Erm, I hate to wear this old suit to church? It's threadbare! The deacons will be bringing us a care package.

ERMA: Okay, so I'm sorry that I left your blue suit at the cleaners. What else can I say?

FRED: Yeah . . . well . . . I notice you didn't leave your favorite dress at the cleaners! You always look nice. You know I work hard all week and don't have the time to take my own things to the cleaners. You should stay on top of these things, Erm. My mom always told me, "Son, always wear the best you have to the house of God!" How can I obey my poor dead mother when the best I have is locked in at the cleaners? The only way I could wear the best I have is to commit a felony! It's just no way to start worship.

[Fred hits another chuckhole. Milo bounces up and hits the top of the car.]

MILO: Oww! Dad, you're going to kill us all—right on the way to the house of God.

FRED: You wanna drive, Milo?

MILO: Yeah!

FRED: Well, you can't. So be quiet and read your Bible!

ERMA: Milo! Let's keep the peace, what do you say?

DAWN MARIE [singing]: Jesus loves me this I know, for the Bible tells me so, little ones to him belong . . .

FRED: Dawn Marie, don't sing. I've got a headache.

DAWN MARIE: Daddy, why don't you like your brown suit?

FRED: Dawn Marie, I don't want to talk about it now.

MILO: Cool it, Dawn Marie. Don't sing "Jesus Loves Me" anymore either; it makes Daddy nervous when people sing about Jesus and his best suit is locked in the cleaners.

FRED [after a long silence]: You know, Erm, I feel spiritually depleted.

DAWN MARIE: Maybe it's because you're so mad about your suit being at the cleaners, Daddy.

MILO: Maybe it's because we're all facing another one of Pastor Smith's sermons.

ERMA: Well, Pastor Smith sure believes in getting the church funds into work overseas, doesn't he?

FRED: Yes, Erm . . . but every cent? Stu Johnston says the pastor wants to scratch the new church gym and roller-skating rink and give the money to the "monkey eaters."

ERMA: Fred! That's no way to talk about missionaries in front of the children.

MILO: I guess you're right, Mom. Dad should try to protect us and help us have a good view of the missionaries. But when I think about them getting all the money that we should be spending on the new church gym . . .

ERMA: You know what the pastor says, Milo. There are many places in the world where missionaries don't even have a simple school to educate their people . . . let alone a big gymnasium or roller-skating rink.

MILO: Will the new church have a bowling alley?

FRED: It's supposed to . . . and Brunswick equipment, too . . . that is, if we don't give it all to the missionaries.

MILO: Why do the monkey eaters need so much money?

ERMA: Milo, please!

MILO: I mean missionaries!

FRED: I don't know, Milo. I only know that all of us who think charity begins at home better be there next Sunday night and help the pastor get a good view of the bowling ministry we can have right here.

[There is silence for a moment and then Fred hits another hole and swerves to miss still another. There is a lot of jostling in the car but nobody speaks. At last Fred breaks the silence.]

FRED: Erma, do you know why I pay taxes four times a year and why every street on the way to God's house is filled with holes?

ERMA: I don't know, dear, why?

FRED: I don't know why. That's just the point. It leaves me all out of sorts by the time I get to church, especially if you start a fight on the way! Why do you have to start a quarrel on the way to church?

MILO: Well, Dad, here we are. It's time to wipe that ugly frown off your face and start calling Mom "sweetie" for a couple of hours. Let's all open these car doors, step out into the parking lot and watch Godzilla transform!

[Fred growls as he stops the car. The doors fly open and the MacArthurs step out on the church parking lot. A family waves at them as they leave their car and walk over to the MacArthurs. Fred's lips part above his clenched teeth. As his church friends get close he speaks cheerily.]

FRED: Look, honey, it's the Johnstons.

STU JOHNSTON: Hey, Fred, that's a dapper brown suit!

FRED: It's one of my favorites.

MILO: Oh, brother!

FRED: Milo, you take Dawn Marie to her Sunday-school class.

[Milo grabs Dawn Marie's little hand and takes her toward the church.]

FRED: Erma, darling, why don't we sit with the Johnstons in church this morning?

STU [aside to Fred]: Pastor Smith's won over another trustee. Now the building committee wants to scratch the Brunswick bowling center. Fred, I wish they could just see that if we all trusted God a little more, we could win this whole city to the faith and God would literally pave the kingdom with hardwood bowling lanes.

FRED: Stu, you are absolutely on target! I'm sure the pastor thinks he's right. We should be giving more money to missions. But missions is people and people like to bowl, and if we sort of stack the pins in God's favor, what can it hurt? I'll tell you one thing, we all need to go to this church business conference next Sunday night and be sure that the bowling center gets all the attention it deserves. I know once the pastor understands, he'll see how bowling and missions can work together.

STU: I dunno, Fred. He's got his mind made up, and the bowling center isn't in the make-up.

In many ways he doesn't really fit Tranquility Community

Church. He doesn't understand us, does he? Besides, have you noticed that he wears that same gray suit every week? Why, Fred? Why?

FRED: Maybe we should pay the man better.

STU: No—I don't think so. The man just isn't a good manager of his money. In fact, he's overpaid now. This one-suit business has nothing to do with his salary level—it's like he thinks he's a monk or something—like he's taken a vow of poverty. Fred, our church is full of dress-for-success types and we need a pastor who . . .

FRED [interrupting]: Cool it, Stu. Here he comes!

STU: Oh! Hello, Pastor.

FRED: Good morning, Pastor.

PASTOR: Good morning, Fred. Nice looking suit.

FRED: Thanks, Pastor. It's one of my favorites. Got a good one ready this morning, Pastor?

PASTOR: I dunno, Fred! I thought I'd speak on our obligation to let Christ be the unseen guest in our homes. See you in the sanctuary! [Goes on.]

STU: See, he's a funny man, Fred! Christ an unseen guest? One week from the business meeting and he isn't even going to mention the building program? He seems to feel no obligation to build a Brunswick bowling center to reach the masses. I mean, where's the man's priorities?

FRED: Okay, Stu, so he doesn't like bowling. Does that mean he doesn't fit our congregation?

STU: But that same one mindless suit every Sunday, Fred! Don't you see it's all tied together? If you don't dress for success, you don't inspire success, you don't bowl for success. You are a dinosaur or alien! You don't fit the city . . .

FRED: Let's talk about it later.

# Scene II

# Burger Doodle Brouhaha

[Fred slams the car door as he and Erma leave church. Milo sits quietly and Dawn Marie is terrified. Fred starts the car and revs the motor too loud. The car jerks into gear and the tires squeal on the asphalt of the church parking lot. Everyone continues sitting silently. Fred yells at a car in front of him.]

FRED: *Road hog!*

ERMA: Take it easy, Fred. Dawn Marie will have whiplash!

FRED: Well, what did he mean by that?

ERMA: Who? What did *who* mean by *what?*

FRED: Pastor Smith! That's who! Who does he think he is? I think I'm a good example to my children. [Once again, Fred burns rubber as he flies across an intersection in anger.] Erma, you haven't been talking to the pastor's wife about our home life, have you? He sounded pretty specific.

MILO: Yeah, it was like he'd been looking in our windows!

FRED: Knock it off, Milo.

ERMA: Really, Fred! I'm sure Pastor Smith was just preaching his sermon.

FRED: Well, why did he put that part in about dads that scream at their kids and act immature when they don't get their way around the house?

MILO: Yeah, that was a really neat part of the sermon, Dad!

FRED: I told *you* to knock it off, Milo!

ERMA: Really, Fred.

FRED: Erma, I resent his insinuation in that sermon. Is he implying that I don't love my family like Christ loved the church?

ERMA: He didn't have you in mind specifically. There's probably a lot of husbands in church that need to be more loving to their families. You mustn't feel like he was delivering his whole sermon just to you.

FRED: Well, he kept looking right at me. Especially when he said that fathers ought to spend more time with their children. If he didn't mean me, Erm, why did he keep looking right at me? If he meant Sam, why didn't he look at Sam? I tell you, he kept looking at me just like he meant it for me alone!

MILO: I think he meant you, Dad.

ERMA: Milo! [A moment of silence ensues.] Fred, I think you're taking this too personally. I think you're a little paranoid about the whole thing. Sermons aren't really good unless they speak directly to us and we feel something of the burden of their correction.

FRED: Well, Erm, how could he know all of that stuff about me!

ERMA: Fred, it isn't *just* you! It's the Bible. Pastor Smith didn't write the Bible. He just preaches it. I've always believed that if the shoe fits, we should try to wear it. If the Bible addresses our sins, we ought to let the Bible correct our lives.

MILO: You know what I think? I think God helps Pastor Smith see right down inside our evil hearts, and it's kind of like a vision. 'Cause he sees what we are really like and then he just tells the whole congregation, right down to the last dirty, rotten detail of our lives. I mean, let's face it, Dad, the pastor described you to a tee. It was kinda like he was a witch doctor or something.

FRED: That's it—Milo!

ERMA: Don't be so harsh with your son, Fred.

DAWN MARIE [singing]: Jesus loves the little children, all the children of the world . . .

ERMA: That's sweet, Dawn Marie.

DAWN MARIE: We learned it in Sunday school. Know what else we learned in Sunday school?

ERMA: What, Dawn Marie?

DAWN MARIE: We learned that daddies should love their children and play with them and take them to see *Cinderella* and things.

FRED [calming down]: I'm sorry, Dawn Marie. I'm sorry, Erm. But don't you think it's dangerous when Pastor Smith gets the kids to talking about the weaknesses of their fathers and then preaches on it in the church service? Is it right for him to make daddies the whipping posts of the congregation?

ERMA: Still, Fred, I don't think we should criticize the pastor in front of the children. He was just preaching the Word of God. If you wanna get mad, Fred, you will just have to get mad at the Bible.

FRED: Get mad at the Bible? Erma, be realistic. People shouldn't get mad at the Bible. They should listen to it and obey it.

MILO: Wow, now you're gettin' the idea, Dad! Pastor Smith makes a lot of sense sometimes!

FRED: Yeah, Milo, I guess so . . . except when he starts talking about missions. But Milo, if we give a man like Smith his way, the natives of Bongo Bongo will have all our money, and they'll be building bowling centers, and we won't have any way to reach the people here in America whose money creates missions. Is that what we really want, Milo?

MILO: Well, I'll admit I sure would like to see us get that new gym and roller rink, Dad!

ERMA: Well, Milo, I don't know. Maybe we ought to pray about that. Maybe the pastor is right.

FRED [roaring]: *Pray?* [simmering down again] I mean, pray? Erma, prayer has its place, but God helps them that help themselves.

ERMA: *Those,* Fred.

FRED: God helps *those* that help themselves! Well, I'll tell you, there are *those* who are tired of talking prayer and have started talking war in this church. A few of us in this congregation are going to start taking some specific actions.

ERMA: What do you mean, Fred?

FRED: I mean Stu Johnston, Harry Argus, King Sizemore and I are going to meet at Bo-Bo's Pies tomorrow night and see if we can keep this church moving ahead. We love the pastor and we only want to do what is right, but we don't want the monkey eaters of Bongo Bongo getting a bowling center at our expense.

ERMA: Tomorrow night! But Fred, you promised to take Dawn Marie to see *Cinderella.*

FRED: I know, Erma, but the Lord's work comes first.

MILO: Pastor Smith just said in the sermon that the home comes before the church! He said that fathers ought to spend more time with their kids.

FRED: Ah, look Erm, Milo, Dawn Marie . . . I love you all, and I'll spend some time with Dawn Marie and all of you later. But this situation is critical. Not one of our major committees agrees with Pastor Smith. And why can't he dress for success? What's this one-suit thing?

DAWN MARIE [singing]: Jesus loves the little children, all the children of the world.

FRED: Dawn Marie, can't you sing about itsy bitsy spiders?

DAWN MARIE: Sure, Daddy, but Mrs. Smith said that it's right to sing about children in other lands 'cause Jesus loves them so much!

FRED: Oh, okay. I'm sure you're right.

MILO: What can it hurt, Dawn Marie? Let's try the "Itsy Bitsy Spider." This Jesus stuff makes Dad nervous.

DAWN MARIE [singing]: The itsy bitsy spider went up the water spout. . . . Oh, . . . look, Dad! There's the Burger Doodle. Could we eat lunch there today?

FRED: Uh, . . . you got those coupons, Erm?

ERMA: I think so, Fred. [rifles through her purse] Yes . . . yes, here they are!

DAWN MARIE: Oh, goody, Daddy!

[Fred pulls the car into the Burger Doodle lot. All the MacArthurs leave the car, enter the restaurant and stand in line to order.]

FRED: Erma, where are those double-deal coupons?

ERMA: Here, dear. [Erma hands him the burger discount coupons.]

MILO: Now we can all four eat for $3.95. You know, Dad, the Johnstons all go to the Bontemps Cafeteria. I'll bet they spend $3.95 each . . . the saps!

DAWN MARIE: Daddy, do you think someday we could all go to the cafeteria like the Johnstons and eat?

FRED: Someday, Dawn Marie.

MILO: Maybe when the Bontemps has coupons in the paper.

FRED [arriving at the head of the serving line]: I'll have two Double Doodles, a small Dipsy Doodle and a fishwich for the little lady, four fries and Cokes. [The waitress rings it all up on the cash register.] Here are my coupons out of the paper.

WAITRESS: I'm sorry, sir. These coupons expired on Wednesday.

FRED: There must be some mistake.

MILO: There goes the cheepo-deepo lunch for your loved ones, Dad!

FRED: Erma, do you have any other coupons?

ERMA: I'm sorry, Fred.

FRED: Oh, all right. How much, miss?

WAITRESS: Seven dollars and eighty-five cents.

FRED: *Seven dollars and eighty-five cents!*

DAWN MARIE: Momma, can I have a whirla sundae and a fried pie?

MILO: You gotta coupon, Dawn Marie?

DAWN MARIE: Nope.

MILO: Sorry, Dawn Marie, no gotta coupon, no getta pie. It's like Daddy said, *"Seven dollars and eighty-five cents!"*

[The MacArthurs all take their seats in a nearby booth and begin unloading the boxed burgers and fries and paper cups.]

MILO: Oh, look, here's somebody else's mustard drying on our table.

ERMA: Well, just wipe it off, dear.

MILO: It won't come off. It's been here for three Sundays now.

DAWN MARIE: Oh, it's all dried and cracked and yikky.

FRED: Erma, remember that the missionary we had from Somalia a couple of months ago? Do you think he was telling the truth about world hunger?

ERMA: Well, why wouldn't he be, Fred?

FRED: Maybe to get a lot of money, Erma. Everybody who comes to our church begs for money. I just can't believe that so many people are going without food overseas.

DAWN MARIE: Did their coupons expire, Daddy?

FRED [choking on a bit of burger]: No, Dawn Marie, they are all hungry because of drought and famine—at least that's what the preacher says.

DAWN MARIE: My teacher said we should all pray for them and give them money so they can buy rice. We're going to take up a collection in Sunday school for the poor children in Smallia.

ERMA: So-mal-ia, Dawn Marie.

DAWN MARIE: Som-alia. Our teacher showed us pictures of some little children just like us with almost no clothes and big stomachs. She said they had no food and many of them died.

MILO: That's why we are taking up an offering for world hunger. Our teacher said that if we gave up just one ticket to the football game, we could feed a whole family for a month. These families have almost no income at all!

FRED: Well, maybe if your ticket was for a championship game on the fifty-yard line or in one of the boxes . . . I don't know. Last year when Sam Zuchowsky was laid up for three months, he had no income and he made it just fine.

MILO: Just think, Dad. If we gave up our season tickets to the Bushwackers, we could feed an entire family in Somalia for a year, I bet.

FRED: That's not a reasonable solution, Milo. Where is your sense of priorities? We are not giving up our season tickets to the Bushwackers. If Sam Zuchowsky made it, so can those people overseas.

ERMA: I don't know, Fred. It's different over there. Only seven per cent of the ground raises crops and the population is still growing.

FRED: Well, when they quit having so many kids, I'll give up my Bushwacker pass. When they make some sacrifices, I'll make some. Besides, I read where many of those overseas relief programs get siphoned off into the black market.

DAWN MARIE: Momma, what's the black market?

ERMA: It's . . . uh . . . where certain commodities . . . get stolen or sold . . .

DAWN MARIE: How can a comedy be stolen?

ERMA: Com-*mod*-ity. It's like grain or cheese or . . . [abruptly] Fred, I forgot to mention that I felt compelled last month to pledge $100 for relief in Somalia.

FRED: You *what?* Erma, are you crazy? "Charity begins at home." That's what my old uncle always said. "God helps them that help themselves!" We don't even know anybody in Somalia.

DAWN MARIE [sipping her Coke]: Daddy, Jesus once fed five thousand people and I'll bet he didn't know them very well. They probably had a lot of babies too, Daddy, but Jesus just fed them and their babies. Mommy, do you think we could do something to help the Zuchowskys?

MILO: I don't know, they've got seven children! Maybe when they quit having babies, Dawn Marie. You know Dad, he doesn't like to help people with babies.

DAWN MARIE [singing]: Jesus loves the little children . . .

# S c e n e III

# The Miracle Marriage Seminar

[Fred and Erma, having just had a tiff over an anniversary that Fred forgot, have decided to attend a Miracle Marriage Seminar recommended by Harry and Lettie Argus, whose own marriage was deep in trouble and saved by an M.M. weekend three years before. The first seminar has ended and Fred and Erma have just settled into a smaller B and B group—Bug and Blessing discussion group. Lettie and Harry are their B and B group leaders.]

KING SIZEMORE: Fred, before this next Miracle Marriage Seminar session gets underway, can you tell me if you're still committed to the course of action we decided at Bo-Bo's Pies last Tuesday?

FRED: Sort of. I just want to be sure we do what's right for Tranquility Community Church.

ERMA: That's sweet, Fred!

KING: Maybe sweet. Maybe spineless!

ERMA: Fred, do you think that is what the pastor was trying to say in his sermon last week?

FRED: Really, Erm? I can't remember what he said.

ERMA: But Fred, you were terribly disturbed all through lunch at the Burger Doodle. Remember? He said that a husband was a guardian of his family, a servant to his children and a model of the Christian life . . .

FRED: Never mind, Erma. I do remember.

ERMA: Fred, I'm wondering if we all are not taking this crusade to build the Christian Life Center a little too seriously. Maybe we all need to think through our relationship with our church and pastor a little more. I've been wondering if we can ever have any bigness in our lives if we don't see the whole world while living in our corner of it. Do we really need this gymnasium?

KING: Erma, it's far more than just a gym. It's a roller rink and a Brunswick bowling center too. All in all it's a tool to reach the athletically inclined for Jesus!

ERMA: Still, we all have so many blessings, and yet the more that God gives us the more we want for ourselves. Is it possible our whole church is filled with self-seeking Christians who live indulgent lives? Are we that way? Do we care so much for Christian bowling alleys that we can't see the world around us dying without a crust of bread?

FRED [a long silence]: It's apples to oranges, Erm. Your comparison doesn't fit at all . . .

ERMA: Are you sure? Just be sure you're doing the right thing, Fred. That's all I ask.

STU: It's right to succeed. It's right to reach out to the community, and we're not doing that! We're going to get this church turned around, Erma, that's all! What did you think of the pastor's sermon last Sunday, King?

KING: Well, to be honest, Stu, I just don't think the pastor has a leg to stand on. He never once mentioned submission as the joyous service of women. He needs to speak out more on the man as the head of the home! That's the Bible way!

HARRY [calling the meeting to order]: All right, let's get started. We hope you've enjoyed our Miracle Marriage Seminar so far. I want each of you to feel very much at ease and just spill out whatever is bugging you in your marriage. Remember now, this is a Bug and Blessing session, and we want you to be up front about the bugs and blessings of your marriage.

How about it, ladies? How about those socks he never quite gets down the laundry chute? Does that bug you? You wanna use rubber gloves and put them on the end of a long stick? Haaaaa!

ERMA [whispering to Fred]: He sounds like he's been loitering at our bedroom door!

FRED [whispering back]: I'll be! That hypocrite! Harry never picks up his socks. The ones at the bottom of his golf bag smell like a mausoleum after an earthquake.

ERMA [still whispering]: All I know is what you do that bugs me, Fred . . .

HARRY: No whispering, you two. [class laughter; Fred turns red] Let's get it out in the open, Fred. You have a little trouble getting your socks down the laundry chute?

FRED: What's it to ya, Harry?

ERMA: Fred! [dropping back to a whisper] You don't have to be so defensive.

HARRY: Does that bug you, Erm? Or is it a blessing, haaaa!

ERMA: Well, I . . .

JANE SIZEMORE: Wanna know what bugs me, Harry?

HARRY: Now we're talking!

JANE: We have a forty-gallon water heater. Every morning King Kong, here, takes a forty-gallon shower and leaves me only the ice water at the bottom of the tank.

KING: It makes your cheeks rosy. [whispering to Jane] Don't be so outspoken. You know you should be more submissive—remember Ephesians 5:22 . . .

JANE: I will not be shushed . . . And that's another thing, Harry. King always tells me to be submissive and quotes Scripture to have his way.

KING: I deny that. [whispering to Jane] "Let your women keep silence in the churches"—1 Corinthians 14:34.

LETTIE: Try quoting "Be ye kind one to another"—Ephesians 4:32, Jane. We used to go to a church where they had a ceremony every year where the women came forward and crowned their husbands lord of the home. I told Harry I'd crown him all right!!! [laughter] In those days Harry quoted a lot of Scripture, and I just told him never to forget that he was no peach.

KING: Just a minute, Harry. You don't have to take that! What about Proverbs 21:9? "It is better to dwell in a corner of the housetop than with a brawling woman in a wide house."

FRED [loudly]: Amen! And what about, "Hell hath no fury like a woman scorned"?

ERMA [whispering]: Fred, I don't think that's in the Bible.

FRED [whispering to Erma]: Of course it is, listen to this. [loudly to the class] 1 Hezekiah 7:3.

ERMA: Fred, I don't think so.

HARRY: All right, folks, let's get back to Bug and Blessing time. What really bugs you in your relationship?

ALFIE [shyly]: My wife talks too loud in public.

MAXINE: *That's a lie, Alfie. My mother told me not to marry you.* I'm sick and tired of your same old complaint: *Maxine always talks too loud and too much. Well, I'll tell you something, Alfie, when someone like you gets critical nobody listens!*

LETTIE: Hey, hey, hey, now you two! Now class, let's work with Alfie and Maxine just a moment. How do you perceive their CF?

ERMA: What's a CF?

FRED [whispering]: Don't ask questions, Erma. It makes you

look dumb.

LETTIE: Compatibility Factor.

KING: Maxine needs to be more submissive. Remember Proverbs 27:15, "A continual dropping in a very rainy day and a contentious woman are alike." I think their CF would be better if Maxine would be a little meeker. The meek shall inherit the earth—Matthew 5:5.

JANE: It isn't the earth that the meek get, King. It's the dirt. Believe me, I know. You should try to be a little more like Alfie; it would improve our CF.

KING: *That worm?* "If a man know not how to rule his own house, how shall he take care of the church of God?"—1 Timothy 3:5.

ERMA: I think their CF would improve if Maxine would talk a little more quietly and respect Alfie's advice. Besides, it can't help but violate the HIM Principle of Relationship.

ALFIE: What's the HIM Principle?

ERMA: The Honor-in-Marriage Principle.

MAXINE: Look, Alfie. If you want to know what it means, read the Manual on Miracle Marriage. Why do you think they mailed us the material three weeks early, Bozo? You'd be surprised at how much your CF will improve if you'd do a little home study!

HARRY: Now, now, Maxine, let's all try to be a little more healing in these sessions. Fred, what do you think of Alfie's HIM Principle as opposed to Maxine's?

FRED: I think that Maxine should be more submissive, just like Erma.

MAXINE: Erma isn't submissive. She's whipped, Fred. You've made a houseplant out of the woman.

LETTIE: Okay, okay, I tell you what. Let's all break into two-somes and spend a little QIC time.

FRED: CF I know. And HIM I know; but what's QIC time?

MAXINE: Read the material, Bozo!

FRED: Look, Maxine, you're married to Bozo. My name is MacArthur.

LETTIE: Okay . . . okay . . . okay! QIC is Quality in Communication. Each of you get together and spend the next hour with your mates and write down a list of your Mutual Enjoyment Resources.

ERMA: Just think, Fred, after our MER list is complete, we will be just that much closer to establishing a more routine QIC and then our CF should improve our whole HIM evaluation. This is so exciting!

FRED: Sheesh!

KING: PTL. "For this cause shall a man leave father and mother, and shall cleave to his wife and they twain shall be one flesh"— Matthew 19:5.

FRED: King, do you think Pastor Smith has studied all this QIC stuff?

KING: Quality in Communication? You gotta be kidding, Fred! Smith is a poor communicator—and yet the Bible says that the man of God should be a good Bible teacher—1 Timothy 3:2.

FRED: Do you know of any Scriptures that teach we ought to give all our money to missions overseas while we do without those very things that would help us get more people who could then give even more money for overseas work?

KING: Fred, I believe we are all supposed to care for those around us first.

FRED: Is there a Scripture that says just that, King? Our whole Christian Life Center could depend on it.

KING: I'm sure there is, Fred. I'll try to find it by the next board meeting.

ERMA: I'm sure you will.

# Scene IV

# Dying Brain Cells and Living Churches

[It is Saturday morning just before breakfast. The phone rings. Erma answers.]

ERMA: Hello! . . . Yes, this is Erma, King. . . . Well, King I knew it was you because I've said hello to you a good many times. How's Jane? . . . I'm sorry. Something she ate? . . . Tell her she mustn't let this business at church get her down. I know Fred is awfully upset too, but, of course, I think we all need to become more positive. I wanted to talk to Jane about it, King; after all, we women should take more part in these controversies. What? . . . 1 Corinthians 14:34? I can't recall right now . . . Oh, that . . . yes . . . well, I'm sure you want to talk to Fred . . . *Fred! It's King!*

FRED [comes to the phone]: Hello, King! What's up? . . . Sure I'll support you at the business conference! . . . You're going to what?

Well, I don't know. . . . Yes, I know I said I'd support you, but I'm not sure. . . . This seems pretty drastic. [pause] Yes, I would like to save the Christian Life Center and the Brunswick bowling equipment. . . . Well, okay, if both Stu and Harry are in on it, count me in too. . . . Yes, okay. I'll see you in the morning at church. Yes, good-bye, King. Thanks for calling.

[Milo emerges from the bathroom with his toothbrush stuck in his jaw, drooling white. Dawn Marie is sitting at the breakfast table all starched and pretty and ready for whatever adventure her Saturday may offer.]

FRED: Oh, it looks like breakfast is ready. [Fred notices Milo brushing and foaming near the hall door.] Milo, hurry up. We're still waiting to say grace. Milo, go back to the bathroom to brush your teeth—get a move on—we're going to have to say the prayer without you.

[Milo retreats back toward the bathroom.]

DAWN MARIE: Momma, can I pray?

ERMA: All right, dear.

FRED: Sit down, Erm. God doesn't like it when you fiddle in the icebox when the little children are trying to pray.

[Erma sits down.]

ERMA: Okay, Dawn Marie.

DAWN MARIE: *Let us pray.* [She bows her head and clamps her eyes tightly, wrinkling her face into distortion.] For these and other blessings . . .

MILO [yelling from the bathroom]: Mom, where's my Izod shirt?

DAWN MARIE: . . . we are about to receive . . .

ERMA [yelling back]: Look in the basket by the dryer, Milo.

FRED: Erm, for pity's sake, Dawn Marie is talking to God.

DAWN MARIE [never opening her eyes, praying even louder]: . . . may the Lord make us truly thankful.

MILO [yelling from the downstairs]: It's not in the laundry basket, Mom!

DAWN MARIE: Bless Mommy and Uncle Harry . . .

ERMA [yelling back]: Milo, did you look under your tube socks?

FRED: Erm, for pity's sake, the kid's praying.

DAWN MARIE: And bless Milo and help him find his Izod shirt, AAAA-MEN.

ERMA: Amen. Thanks, Dawn Marie.

FRED: Amen.

MILO [yelling back from upstairs]: Hey, Mom, I found it.

DAWN MARIE: Mom, do you think God answers everybody's prayers that fast?

FRED: Pass the eggs, Erm.

ERMA: God always answers prayers.

FRED: These eggs are terrible . . . they're cold.

MILO [running in and taking his chair]: Hi, Dad. Hi, Mom. Hi, Dawn Marie. I'm ready to say grace.

DAWN MARIE: I already said it, Milo.

FRED: How do you think you found your shirt? It's Dawn Marie's first miracle of the day.

MILO: Well, I see Dad's in his usual jovial mood.

DAWN MARIE: Mom, the pastor says we ought to read the Bible after breakfast as a family. Can we?

ERMA: What do you think, Fred?

FRED: *I* think the eggs are cold.

ERMA: I think you better eat them before they get colder.

DAWN MARIE: Maybe we can start reading the Bible at breakfast tomorrow. Okay, Mom?

ERMA: Maybe, Dawn Marie. You can go shopping with me in a half-hour or so, if you would like.

DAWN MARIE: Oh, goodie!

ERMA: So as soon as you finish eating, maybe you ought to go up and straighten your room.

DAWN MARIE: Okay, Mommy. Could I look at the pictures in my Bible story book since we didn't have time to read the Bible together like the pastor said?

ERMA: Okay, dear. Run along now and straighten your room [Exit Dawn Marie.] Fred, what did King Sizemore want?

FRED: King? Oh, nothing.

ERMA: What didn't you want to support him on?

FRED: Oh, nothing, Erm. . . . It's nothing!

ERMA: Well, whatever this "nothing" is it sure seemed to upset you. Sounds like King, Stu and Harry are all in on this "nothing" too.

FRED: We've got to do it. The pastor needs to be held in check. His priorities are all scrambled. We want to see our church grow and it's never gonna happen as long as Pastor Smith sees all the needs as being somewhere other than our own community. We've got to do what we've got to do. Don't question me. Just trust me.

ERMA: All right, Fred. But I think we'd all be better off if we began to try to understand the pastor instead of taking matters into our own hands.

FRED: Well, Erma, we've all tried to be understanding. Nothing has helped! Now we have to do something more concrete. We've got to take action. Besides, you know how well King Sizemore knows the Bible. He just reminded me on the phone that Jesus taught the disciples to minister first to Jerusalem and then the uttermost parts of the earth—Acts 1:8 or 8:1 or something like that. Anyway, if King says the pastor is out of line, then I think we ought to consider his godly advice.

ERMA: But, Fred, just because King Sizemore reads the Bible a lot doesn't mean he is godly!

FRED: Of course he is, Erma! He says that there's a preacher in California with eight thousand members. And do you know what they started their church with? A gymnasium and a Brunswick bowling center, and now they have to have paid parking attendants on Sunday just to handle all the cars. We just don't have a success mentality at our church! Pastor Smith wants to give all the money overseas while our poor little church sits here withering. We feed natives ten thousand miles away who can't even spell Brunswick. We've got to stop this defeated thinking! We give *our* money to this church too, Erma, and we ought to have a say. How much money did we give last year? How much, I ask you?

ERMA: Seventy-seven dollars and fifty-three cents, I think, Fred.

FRED [growing quiet]: Oh, I thought it was more than that. Are you sure, Erma?

ERMA: Yes, I remember for sure. I thought at the time that it wasn't very much. It averages about a buck forty-nine a week. . . . How much does it cost for a line of bowling? . . . I mean, with automatic pin setters and all?

FRED [changing the subject]: Well, okay so we're not the Rockefellers, but I think everyone would give more if we had a nice facility for basketball and bowling, and I intend to have it, even if . . .

ERMA: Even if what, Fred?

FRED: Never mind. Take Dawn Marie shopping. . . . Seventy-seven dollars and fifty-three cents? Are you sure? You wouldn't happen to remember what we spent on our season tickets for football, would you?

ERMA: I sure would, Fred, it was . . .

FRED: Never mind, Erma. I think I'll go rake the lawn.

DAWN MARIE [running back into the room holding something behind her]: Mommy, my room is straight now. Mommy, tomorrow is Sunday-school day!

ERMA: That's right, honey. . . . What are you holding behind you? You haven't got Milo's tarantula, do you, Dawn Marie?

DAWN MARIE [smiling]: . . . uh . . .

ERMA: Fred, Fred, she's got Milo's tarantula! Fred, make her put it back!

FRED: Dawn Marie, you put Milo's tarantula back right now! You know it terrifies your mother.

DAWN MARIE: Here's what I got, Daddy! [Dawn Marie extends Fred's Bible.]

MILO: Dawn Marie! You know how Bibles terrify your father. It makes him feel guilty about not going to Sunday school.

FRED [throws down the Bible in disgust]: I don't care what you say, Milo. Sunday school is for kids. I have no intention of trying to learn all this stuff when I'm a grown man! I'm forty-two, for Pete's sake!

ERMA: Well, you never get too old to learn, Fred. What do you say we try Sunday school?

MILO: Correction, Mother. Dad *may* be too old. I read that after thirty-five your brain cells start to die.

DAWN MARIE: Daddy . . .

FRED: Yes, dear.

DAWN MARIE: When your brain cells start to die do your hair cells start to die too? [Fred looks annoyed as Dawn Marie continues.] I just wanted to know 'cause the other day there was this gray stuff in the shower drain, Daddy, after you took your shower and . . .

MILO: Oh, Dawn Marie, that gray stuff is just gunk. Brain cells don't wind up in shower drains. They just grow hard and rocky and stay in your head.

ERMA: That's enough, children. Can't you see your father is irritated? [changing the tone of her voice and speaking directly to Fred] Honey, don't you think that it would be a good example to the children if you went to Sunday school with them instead of just dropping them off?

MILO: There's a great idea! Dad, why don't you try becoming a good example for us children? Let's all go to Sunday school together tomorrow.

FRED [clearly exasperated]: Not on your life! They call my group the Harmony Class. Some harmony they have. They took the first thirty minutes of class to decide whether they should have a progressive dinner in February or a potluck in March. They almost got into a fight over the whole subject!

ERMA: Well, dear, what were they supposed to be studying?

FRED: The book of Collisions, I think.

ERMA: Colossians, Fred!

MILO: Mom, Dad doesn't need Sunday school. It's for kids.

DAWN MARIE: Can you name the twelve apostles, Daddy?

ERMA: Sure he can, Dawn Marie. Don't bother your father now. You can see he's upset about the whole subject of Sunday school.

DAWN MARIE: I know this song, Daddy, that helps me remember all twelve of them in exact order. [Dawn Marie begins singing.] Peter, Andrew, James . . .

MILO: I get the next three, Dawn Marie. [Milo begins singing.] And John, Philip and Bartholomew . . . Okay, Mom, your turn.

ERMA [smiling, she begins to sing]: Thomas, Matthew, James the Less . . .

MILO: Okay, Dad, it's your turn.

FRED: You guys got all the easy ones . . . let's see . . .

MILO: Why don't you try Harry, Stu and King Sizemore?

DAWN MARIE [grinning from ear to ear, begins singing and finishes the list]: Thaddeus, Simon, Judas . . . That's the last three, Daddy, now you try the song.

ERMA: Never mind, Dawn Marie . . . not now at least. Daddy doesn't know the twelve apostles.

DAWN MARIE: Is that because he won't go to Sunday school?

MILO: I think it's 'cause his brain cells are dying.

FRED: Well, I have never heard Tom Anderson sing that song, and I'll bet Joe Clinton doesn't know all the twelve apostles. And both of them go to that Bible study, that Harmony Class each week.

MILO: Well, at least they're good examples to their kids.

ERMA: There is a lot to be said for going to Sunday school each week. [Erma turns her back on Milo, seeing that Fred is near a breaking point.] Maybe we could try a new class where they don't take so much of the Bible study time to plan potlucks. At least we'd all be learning together. And it is important to keep learning about the Bible.

DAWN MARIE: I love the Bible, Daddy. I know another song that has all the books of the Old Testament in it. Wanna hear it, Daddy? [Dawn Marie begins singing.] Genesis, Exodus, Leviticus, Numbers . . . Momma, you think this song is too hard for Daddy?

ERMA: I think so, Dawn Marie. Your daddy doesn't want to try to learn the books of the Old Testament right now. You see, he's tired and . . .

MILO: And he's a poor example to us kids, and his brain cells are dying. . . . Dad, there's this doctor that spoke at a Christian Youth chapter meeting, and he said that churches are like bodies made up of many cells and that some of the cells are in the head and some in the feet.

FRED: No sermons, Milo. I've got a tension headache.

MILO: And he said that the head of the body is Christ and that if some of the cells begin to fight with other cells that the head can't direct the body. He said it's like leukemia where the cells in the blood all take sides and fight against each other until the body becomes very weak, and it can finally die, and then the head cannot have any effect on the body at all.

FRED: Erma, could I have a couple of aspirin?

ERMA: I'll get them, dear. Milo, Dad has a bad headache. Maybe you had better not try to preach anymore to him. [exit]

MILO: And when finally all the cells have killed each other there really can't be any life in the body at all. Know what he said kills most churches? Civil war. He said that most churches don't or-ganize to fight sin or evil in the world. They just all choose up sides and fight each other. This doctor said he had a patient that once weighed two hundred pounds and finally got down to under a hundred because his body was at war with itself. He said that humility of spirit and a strong concept of God's love was about all that could cure spiritual leukemia in the church.

FRED: *Enough. Cool it, Milo!*

MILO: Okay, okay. But tomorrow night is the big business conference, and if you don't mind I'd just like to ask you one question, Dad.

FRED: Oh, all right, I guess.

MILO: Okay. Tell me, Dad, are you a healthy cell or are you a cancerous, warmongering cell?

FRED: I . . . I . . .

ERMA [re-entering]: Here are your aspirin, Fred. [Fred gulps the aspirin.] You know, Fred, I found a most interesting verse in our Sunday-school lesson for tomorrow.

FRED: What is it, Erm?

ERMA: Oh, I'm sure it has no significance to us. . . . Still . . .

FRED: What is it, Erm?

ERMA: I don't know, Fred . . . It seems somehow too direct . . .

FRED: *What is it, Erm?*

ERMA: It's Galatians 5:15.

FRED: What does it say?

ERMA: "If ye bite and devour one another, take heed that ye be not consumed one of another."

MILO: Wow, Mom! Read that again!

FRED: Never mind, Erma. My head is splitting.

MILO: Sometimes it's heads and sometimes it's churches, Dad.

# Scene V

# Long Meetings and Short Prayers

PASTOR [standing to his feet]: We have been arguing about this Christian Life Center long enough. Maybe we ought to pray about it.

STU: Pastor, I'm sorry, but we all think that there's a time when prayer is action and a time when it is a substitute for action! Let's all get honest with our Lord and lay our cards on the table. We want to know, are you for this new Christian Life Center or not?

PASTOR: It is a good thing, but . . .

STU: But what?

PASTOR: But is it so important that we want to saddle our church with the kind of debt that might prevent us from dealing with the great needs that exist in the world around us? There are so many who are hungry and poor and without the gospel!

KING: What about the great needs that exist here at home? Never forget that the Scriptures teach "Ye have the poor with you always"—Mark 14:7! Now the lost of Madagascar are no more lost than the lost of our own city. In Madagascar you reach them by buying their lunch: but here you need to reach them by being creative and drawing them to Jesus with a nice building and things like that.

PASTOR: Yes, but remember that in Matthew 25:44 the Bible teaches that we are to see the great needs of the entire world and that in Christ's love we must try to meet those needs with a glass of cold water or a cup of rice!

KING: Now, Pastor, I don't need to remind you that in the early church everybody cared just about those right in the city of Jerusalem. The Scripture says, "Neither was there any among them that lacked: for as many as were possessors of lands or houses sold them, and brought the prices of the things that were sold, and laid them down at the apostles' feet"—Acts 4:34-35. Now if we were to care about those right in our immediate "Jerusalem," then we could have a truly great church and a gymnasium and bowling alley and skating rink that would bring many to Jesus. Out in California, Pastor Gil Roller built a church of eight thousand members, and they started with just a simple gym and a bowling center, lovingly dedicated to Jesus. Now they raise enough each month to feed thousands of poor people.

HARRY: We think we could attract a lot more members if we just had a nice gym and a . . . a . . .

FRED: A bowling center.

HARRY: Yes, thanks, Fred. One with Brunswick automatic pinsetters!

PASTOR: But do we want to attract members with pinsetters?

FRED: Well, if it helps the church grow, what could be better?

PASTOR: Jesus! Oh, I know that sometimes people are drawn to Jesus by using other things, but . . .

KING: Well, why don't we simply try pinsetters? That's all we're asking!

PASTOR: What if we just hold Jesus up to our whole world where there is much suffering and illness and death? I would like to see us as a church become an example to our entire community of the fact that Jesus really is the light of the world. And the world is so dark. Now I'm not opposed to all of these assets; surely Christians have a right to exercise and the good life; but should we build all of these trivial things at the expense of the world beyond our doors?

KING: Well, if that don't beat all! Are you calling this new Christian Life Center a trivial thing? Pastor, don't you know that St. Paul said, "I am made all things to all men that I might by all means save some"—1 Corinthians 9:22?

STU: Brother Wilson, our last pastor, believed in evangelizing those right here at home and using every means to win all he could. He loved Gil Roller's sermons and if he would have stayed more than eighteen months, I'm sure he would have built a church along the same lines as Gil Roller's in . . . in . . .

FRED: Bakersfield?

STU: San Leandro! Do you know what Brother Roller teaches about projects like this? He would say that nothing is too costly if it brings people to our precious Lord. He even sponsors Caribbean cruises to help people grow in Christ. And remember, this bowling center only seems expensive to us because we haven't seen the great resources of God. Whatever we want and ask by faith, believing, we will receive—yes, sir! And we are going to claim this new gymnasium by faith! The whole Christian Life Center . . . Brunswick automatic pinsetters and all. Pastor, we are going to fight for what we believe in—the evangelization of this community. I hope you don't mind, but I've ordered Brother Gil's new book, *Your Church Can Grow If You Believe.* As soon as it's in I'll give it to you. In the meantime, here's Brother Gil's sermon from last week's telecast. It's called "Upward to Power!" [hands pastor a cassette]

PASTOR: Thank you. . . . I guess. . . . Well, we are all through for tonight. Let's conclude our meeting with prayer: Our Father, make us one in love! Amen. [Pastor shakes hands with the board and leaves.]

STU: I don't mean to be critical, but did you fellows hear how short his prayer was? Brother Gil Roller never prays less than five minutes, unless he's giving away a book for contributions. Say, King, I don't know if I should bring this up, but there's a new man graduating from Brother Gil's academy named Ford Forthrightly who is looking for a new church. Do you suppose Pastor Smith's time could be up and maybe the Lord is ready to lead him somewhere else? Brother Gil Roller says many a church is powerless because the pulpit is powerless.

KING: You know, it's been a long time since I've heard Pastor Smith preach on Christian victory. Maybe that's why we're seeing so much turmoil in the church. Maybe this Ferd fellow is worth praying about.

STU: Not Ferd—Ford! Ford Forthrightly! Ferd, I mean, Fred, you're being awfully quiet. What do you think of this crisis?

FRED: I keep thinking about something that my son said about cancerous body cells!

STU: You think maybe Pastor Smith is a cancer in this congregation?

FRED: Maybe . . . I mean, no . . . I mean . . . I don't know what I think . . . I'll see all of you later.

# ACT II

# Scene I

# What Genghis Khan Said to His Father the Night He Left Home

[Fred slams the door and throws his briefcase in the corner. He's a half-hour late for dinner. He goes immediately to the kitchen and growls.]

FRED: I'm starving to death. What's for dinner?

ERMA: Burger Builder casserole.

FRED: What's it building tonight?

ERMA: It's the Polynesian Sweet and Sour Burger Builder.

FRED: I never have liked Burger Builder since you left the box-top in the Spanish rice.

ERMA: Well, you'll like this, Fred. Madge says Harvey loves it. She feeds it to him all the time.

FRED: Harvey is a weasel.

ERMA: Whatever you think of Harvey, Madge says he likes it.

FRED: Harvey likes Alpo—probably 'cause you can't buy weasel food in better stores everywhere.

[Milo enters the kitchen.]

MILO: What smells so good? Dad, can I have the car keys?

FRED: It's Polynesian Sweet and Sour Burger Builder, and no you can't.

MILO: Dad, please. All the gang is counting on me to drive them to the rock concert.

FRED: Well, Milo, you'll just have to tell your little glue-sniffing friends to call Yellow Cab.

ERMA: Please, Fred, what can it hurt?

FRED: It can hurt plenty, Erm. Now don't side with Milo. Remember all those kids that got trampled to death in Dubuque at the Bo-Zo's concert?

ERMA: It was Des Moines, Fred, and this group is not big time.

MILO: Dad, it's Galapagos and the Chi-Chi's, and they're only in town tonight.

FRED: Sit down, Milo, and eat your Burger Builder. Who's gonna say grace?

MILO: Not me! God knows how I feel about Burger Builder.

FRED: Okay, okay, I'll say it! God is good. God is great. God, we thank you for the Burger Builder. [Fred begins coughing and then clears his throat and tries to continue.] God, we truly thank you for this which you have provided. [Again he begins coughing and is unable to finish the blessing.] It's no use, is it, God?

ERMA: Amen!

MILO: Amen!

FRED: Amen!

MILO: Look, Dad, you just gotta give me the car keys.

FRED: Milo, you are not going to drive my car to the Galapagos and the Chi-Chi's concert. And that is final, *final*, FINAL!

ERMA: Fred, please! Your spitting Polynesian!

FRED: Gil Roller says that rock music is one of the signs of the end of times. Milo, do you wanna be with all those glue sniffers when Jesus comes again?

MILO: Dad, he probably won't come tonight. Besides, none of us are glue sniffers! We're good, middle-class American kids. We're not gonna get in trouble.

FRED: That's exactly what Genghis Khan said to his dad when he left home. Milo, I know you don't mean to get into any trouble, but when the marijuana smoke gets thick, you can run into greasy, hairy things in the dark and never see them. It's no place for a *Christian* to be. Besides, what if Jesus did come again?

MILO: Dad, for Pete's sake! Jesus is not coming back tonight, I promise. I'll be careful with the car!

FRED: No!

MILO: Look, Dad, I'm eighteen now and I don't keep *my* teeth in a cup at night. [Fred shifts uneasily and adjusts his dentures.] Galapagos and the Chi-Chi's are great composers. I'll be culturally deprived if I miss this concert. None of our church friends have to know unless you tell them. Besides, last time I went, the deacons' kids were sitting in the best seats.

FRED: No, Milo!!!

MILO [becoming loud]: Well, I'm going anyway! If you think I'm gonna sit around and eat Burger Builder all my life while you listen to Tex Twang and the Tumbleweeds and criticize Galapagos and the Chi-Chi's you're wrong, Dad. *You are wrong, wrong, wrong!* I get no respect around here. Tom's dad doesn't care if Tom goes—even bought him tickets to the concert . . . and I bought my own!

FRED [becoming incensed]: You already got your tickets?

MILO: Dad, this isn't the Buschmeiser Clydesdales! If I hadn't gotten my tickets early, I would never have gotten into the place tonight. I'll see you, Dad. You can have my Burger Builder.

FRED [rising and furious]: All right, you wild kid! [Fred throws the keys] Here are the keys! *Go kill yourself on the freeway for all I care!*

MILO [grabs the keys and runs out of the room]: Thanks, Pops. I'll never forget you for this!

FRED [yelling as he disappears through the door]: Yeah, well I hope Jesus comes back tonight about eight-thirty. It'll serve you right! [He changes his voice tone and turns to Erma.] Erm, you wanna be serving your loved ones Burger Builder when Jesus comes again?

ERMA: Oh, Fred, I almost forgot. This came for you in the mail today.

FRED: A letter! A letter from Pastor Smith! [rips open and reads]

ERMA: Well, what does it say, Fred?

FRED [growing angry, wads the letter up after a studied reading and hurls the missile across the room]: Erma, I can't believe this.

ERMA: What is it, dear? [goes across the room and picks up the wadded letter and unwraps it] Well, it's only a form letter to the congregation. Why in the world would you get so upset?

FRED: Read it, if you can . . .

ERMA: "Dear Member." Well, at least it's not personal . . .

FRED: Just read it, Erm. It isn't enough that my kid likes those rock and roll punks, but my pastor is taking a stand against the only hope I have of reaching Milo. Erm, this man has to be stopped.

ERMA [reading]: "After our board meeting this past week, I am all the more convinced that we cannot hope to teach our children about self-sacrifice and world need while we continue to focus all our attention on a building program that will give us a beautiful but unnecessary facility . . ."

FRED: What can he mean by *unnecessary? Unnecessary in whose view?*

ERMA [continues reading]: "Within a mile of our church there are three community gymnasiums and two bowling alleys. As your pastor I would like you to prayerfully consider that we take the money previously designated for this facility and offer it to two agencies for missions and world famine relief. . . ." Oh, Fred, I know you were counting so wholeheartedly on that Brunswick bowling center.

FRED: Erma, it isn't just me! Most of the men of the church feel the same way! This could be all-out war. When will Pastor Smith learn that you can't lead sheep where they don't want to go?

ERMA: Fred, I remember a visiting pastor saying that often sheep did not know where it was best to go and that they needed to rely on the shepherd. Pastor Smith *is* our shepherd, Fred. Maybe it would be best to let him do the leading, or at least to ask him why he feels the way he does.

FRED: No, Erma. We've been through all this before. It's three weeks till the next board meeting. Somehow we have to stop his wild giveaway of church funds or we'll never reach our community. Why can't the man understand? This is the age of growing churches—big superchurches! Smith is out of sync with our times. Most churches our size already have excellent facilities. Most pastors believe they are necessary to compete with the other big attractions in our city.

Why can't he see this, Erm? Why does our pastor have to be the only one in the whole modern world that sees only the distant lost while he looks past those right here? I think I'll drive over and have a cup of coffee with King Sizemore.

ERMA: Would you want to be having coffee with King if Jesus came tonight at eight-thirty?

# Interlude

MILO: Well, it's film night. I never saw much quality in Christian films. They're low budget, I'm afraid, and all the acting talent you can buy out of the nearest college drama department. The pastor says these missionary films help open our minds to a wider world and, well, I know our pastor gets concerned that more of us don't care about the poor of this world. But I think he gets too worked up over it, myself. Still, his sincerity makes me wonder about life. He speaks with conviction as though he knows the answer. I don't know if there is an answer. Smith always sings the same song—so many Christians here in America while much of the world doesn't even know who Jesus is. I wish the pastor would get off it!

We need this new gym if you ask me. But, of course, you didn't.

Nobody asks me anything! Still we need this gym. I agree with dad—but don't tell him. If we give all our money to Madagascar, we'll never have any for here in America.

Pastor Smith does make me feel guilty though. He says we all throw a tip to God and use our small gifts to salve our conscience. I wish I could get the world off my mind these days. We ought to do something—but I don't see what good it does to go to boring movies at the church. And these movies are not just boring; they're *boring* boring. Mother loves 'em, so we all go.

It's about time for us all to go. Fortunately, they feed us before they bore us—it's only fair. I always eat a lot—it's my only chance to get even!

# Scene II

# Harriet Harding of Haiti— Pioneer!

[Milo is sitting at home in the den while Dawn Marie is reading *Crackers, the Sixteenth Elephant.* Erma has been preparing Burger Builder casserole to take to the church for film night.]

FRED [bursting in the doors]: Hi, honey, I'm home! What's for dinner?

ERMA: It's going to be a feast. We're all going to the church.

FRED: Uh, . . . honey, . . . I don't know. We won't have to listen to Luella Colby talk about the poor people in Madagascar again, will we?

ERMA: It's film night, Fred. And we're all going to enjoy it so much!

DAWN MARIE [yelling so as to interrupt]: Daddy, what's a pakkyderm?

FRED [returning to the den]: I dunno, Dawn Marie. Go look it up.

ERMA [yelling from the kitchen]: Is everybody out there ready?

FRED [yelling back]: How do you get ready for film night, Erma?

MILO: It's an elephant!

FRED: The film or the casserole?

MILO: I was talking to Dawn Marie, Dad!

FRED: What's an elephant, Milo?

DAWN MARIE: Really, Milo? Is an elephant a pakkyderm?

MILO: Yes, Dawn Marie.

DAWN MARIE: Crackers was the sixteenth pakkyderm in the Ringling Brothers, Barnly and Bailey Circus.

MILO: *Barnum* and Bailey, Dawn Marie. . . . Dad, do I have to go to film night?

FRED: Your mother likes 'em, Milo.

MILO: Why, Dad? What's up for tonight?

FRED: It's a real thriller, Milo: *Harriet Harding of Haiti—Pioneer!*

DAWN MARIE: Daddy, what's a proboscis?

ERMA [yelling from the kitchen]: Dawn Marie, come carry the pop bottles to the basement.

DAWN MARIE [yelling ]: Yes, Mother. [quieter] Daddy, what's a proboscis?

FRED: Ask your mother when you carry down the bottles, Dawn Marie.

MILO: It's a trunk, Dawn Marie. Dad, I hate missionary films. Couldn't we go to the video shack and check out *War of the Werewolves?* I have to hold my breath in the school cafeteria on Mondays when the kids are talking about all the neat movies they've seen. I'm always afraid they'll ask me what I've seen. I could just never say I saw *Harriet Harding of Haiti—Pioneer!*

FRED: Tell 'em you saw *Harriet Harding, the Hatchet Hacker!*

MILO: They'd only ask where, and I'd have to tell 'em church.

Dad, there's a million neat movies right now, and *Harriet Harding of Haiti—Pioneer!* is not one of them.

FRED: Well, it should be better than last week's!

MILO: I didn't even go to the lunchroom last Monday. I couldn't tell a soul we all went to see *The Place of Sunday School in Bible Study!* I told Donna Dobson on Tuesday, and now she thinks I'm weird. Know what she said? "You're weird, Milo MacArthur. On Saturday night you go eat Burger Builder with your mother and watch Sunday-school films! You're weird." I could have died, Dad. Know where Donna Dobson was? She was with Charlie the jock watching *Conan Gets Tough!*

ERMA [entering the den with foil-covered casserole]: Well, I'm ready. Everybody ready?

DAWN MARIE [running up from the basement, out of breath]: I'm ready, Mom. Can I take my *Crackers the Elephant* book?

ERMA: No, Dawn Marie. I don't think you'll be able to read when they turn out the lights.

DAWN MARIE: I could sit by the exit light. I can see good there, Mom, when I sit by that little red light.

ERMA: No, Dawn Marie, it wouldn't be good for your eyes.

MILO: I feel sick, Mom.

DAWN MARIE: Me too, Mom!

FRED: They're allergic to noisy projectors, Erma. They should get a patch test. I'll take them first thing next week.

ERMA: Do I sense a little rebellion here?

FRED: Erm, we don't know how to tell you, but it's film night. Every Saturday night it gets worse. What's next week, for pity's sake?

ERMA [begins to whine]: I dunno . . . it's *Good Doctrine, the Key to Biblical Perfection,* I think.

FRED: Oh, Erm. I don't think I can take it. I think I'll take my new *Sports Afield* and read by the exit light . . . if I can find a space.

It's been getting pretty crowded around there.

ERMA [sniffling]: You can't all read around the exit light. You'll go blind.

MILO: Then we can all get big dogs and stay home on film night.

FRED: Milo wants to see *War of the Werewolves*!

ERMA: That's a PG-13 film, isn't it, Milo?

MILO: It's okay. I'm eighteen now, Mom. I got an idea, why don't we all sit down right here and eat the casserole and then we can go and see *The Man from Indiana*. Donna Dobson went with Jim Heffletter and said it was the funniest film she had ever seen.

FRED: Is this the same Donna Dobson that went with Charlie to see *Conan Gets Tough*?

MILO: The girl is popular, Dad. A lot of guys take her to the flicks.

FRED: She doesn't sound like the kind of girl that would go and see *Harriet Harding of Haiti*.

ERMA: *Harriet Harding of Haiti—Pioneer!*

FRED: Yeah, well, whatever. Milo, you stay away from that Donna Dobson. Those kinds of girls go to seamy movies and they love sitting in the dark, watching racy scenes. Yessir, the dark is their bailliwick . . . they get sunburns reading by exit lights. Stay away from this Donna Dobson, do you hear me, Milo?

MILO: I hear you, Dad. What do you say, Mom? Could we eat our Burger Builder here and go to a real movie? You remember what Bill Betterman said about families spending special time together doing things they *all* enjoy? Mom, we don't enjoy film night. Do we, Dad?

FRED: Well, I . . . er . . . well, no, Milo, we don't.

MILO: Dawn Marie?

DAWN MARIE: I wish we could go to real movies like other kids with popcorn and everything.

ERMA: Okay, okay. We'll eat the casserole here, and then we'll go to a real movie.

FRED: Hey, Erm, I tell you what. You freeze it, and we'll eat it later . . . much later! I'm taking all of us to the Burger Doodle for dinner. Got any new coupons?

DAWN MARIE: Hooray, hooray, hooray! We're going to a real movie! Momma, how come we never get to see the projector in a real movie?

MILO: They keep it in the back room, Dawn Marie, and shine it through a hole in the wall.

DAWN MARIE: How come we never see anyone reading by the exit light?

MILO: 'Cause they never show *Harriet Harding of Haiti.*

ERMA: *Harriet Harding of Haiti—Pioneer!,* Milo.

FRED [putting his coat on and preparing to leave with the family]: Erm, several of us were wondering if the church shouldn't give some consideration to selling the manse. It's getting old now and really needs a lot of repairs.

ERMA: But Fred, what would the pastor do? We hardly pay him enough to buy his own house and . . .

FRED: Well, he'd figure out something, I'm sure. He'd probably appreciate it.

ERMA: Honey, the man has enough problems. Maybe we should wait awhile to spring this one on him . . .

FRED: Actually, honey, you're in with Luella Colby and the Madagascar Girls . . . I mean, the Missions Society, and we were wondering if maybe you could give us a little help in . . .

ERMA: Fred, this sounds like a conspiracy of some sort. I'll have absolutely nothing . . .

FRED: Now, now, now, Erma. Let's go to the movie. We don't have to talk about it right now, for goodness' sake.

ERMA: Well, all right! Let's get going.

[The phone rings. Milo answers.]

MILO: Hello. . . . Just a minute. . . . It's for you, Mom!

ERMA: Yes. . . . Oh, hello, Luella. . . . No, we're not coming to film night. Yes, I know that Harriet Harding began the women's prayer movement for the work of Madagascar. . . . Well, we're all going out for the evening to a dinner and . . . if you must know, to a movie, a real movie where they serve popcorn and . . . Mrs. Sizemore said what? *No, I don't care what King said.* I have no intention of serving on any committee to sell the pastor's home. . . . Sure I'll speak to Fred about it, but I'm sure he would never be in favor of selling the pastor's home. The old place isn't much . . . still . . . well, all right, Luella. . . . Yes, certainly, good-bye! [hangs up] Fred, you are in on some sort of plan to sell the parsonage, aren't you?

FRED [clearly nervous]: In on some plan . . . ?

ERMA: Fred . . . are you or aren't you?

FRED: . . . to sell the parsonage . . . ?

ERMA: Fred?

FRED: . . . plan? . . . Er, let's go to the movies, okay?

DAWN MARIE: Do you think what Milo said in the car is right?

ERMA: What's that, Dawn Marie?

DAWN MARIE: That Pastor Smith can see way down deep in our evil hearts?

# Scene III

# Dawn Marie's Slumber Party

[Dawn Marie is having a slumber party, and Fred and Erma are trying to play Monopoly to distract themselves while they stay up with the children. Their minds are not entirely on the game!]

ERMA [rolls dice]: Eight . . . [clicks off spaces with her marker] Great! Marvin Gardens. I'll buy it. That gives me another monopoly.

Now, Fred, I don't want to hear any more about it. I just can't think that this would be a good time to sell the parsonage. I know it's in bad shape, but it doesn't seem fair to Pastor Smith. The timing is all bad. Your roll.

FRED [rolls]: Three. [clicks off spaces with his marker] Maybe this community chest card will be good. . . . Oh, no . . . I pay $150 in school tax. Why do I always get these bum cards? But, Erm, if we keep the parsonage another year we're going to have to spend a fortune in repairs. And I don't think that Pastor Smith . . . I mean, the old house, is worth it.

ERMA:  Fred, you and Stu and King are starting to take yourselves too seriously. We need to call a truce right now on this business. I don't think God would approve of the harrassment of our pastor, especially at a time when the church is in heavy disagreement over the new Christian Life Center.

FRED:  Okay, okay! For pity's sake, we'll talk about it later. Your move, Erma.

ERMA [picks up the dice]:  I already own Park Place. Oh, Lord, give me Boardwalk.

FRED:  No fair invoking divine influence, Erm!

ERMA:  You got Boardwalk the last three times, Fred. [Erma begins to shake the dice vigorously.] Oh, I need a ten . . . a ten . . . please, let me have a ten. . . . [rolls, and the dice thump to a stop]

FRED:  I don't believe it!

ERMA:  Ten! [Erma clicks her marker joyously on the board.] One, two, three, four . . . What are the children doing, Fred?

FRED:  They're watching *Swamp Creatures of Death.*

ERMA:  Five, six, seven . . . *Swamp Creatures of Death*! . . . eight, nine, ten, . . . *Boardwalk.* How much is it, Fred?

FRED:  You know how much it is. Do you want it or not?

ERMA:  Four hundred dollars! Here it is, and I want two hotels.

FRED:  That'll be two thousand more, Erm.

ERMA:  I don't care. Give 'em to me. [She sets the hotels on the game board.] Land on me. This is gonna be my lucky night. I already own three other monopolies and seven hotels. How can I lose?

FRED:  I don't feel much like playin'.

ERMA:  *Swamp Creatures of Death,* did you say? *SWAMP CREATURES OF DEATH!* Isn't that the one where they saw the tentacles off a squid with a chain saw?

FRED: I dunno, Erma. Is it? Is it my roll, Erma? [picks up the dice unenthusiastically] Erma, relax! Our kids can handle a little violence.

ERMA [ignoring Fred]: Fred, lucky you! If you roll a six you'll be on Boardwalk, and I'll be in the chips. Now roll. Don't get a six, Fred, or you'll owe me two thousand bucks.

FRED [shakes the dice and then rolls and watches as the dice thump to a stop]: Darn!

ERMA: Oh . . . Oh . . . *a six! A six!* Oh, goody! Okay, Fred, pay up.

FRED: Erm, I'm flat broke. What if I give you the Light Company and the B & O Railroad?

ERMA: And the "Get Out of Jail Free" card too?

FRED: Okay, okay. But don't get too greedy, Erm. [hearing screaming coming from the next room] I'll bet they're at the scene where they're starting to saw the tentacles off.

DAWN MARIE [running into the room]: Mommy, Sarey just puked on her Artoo Deetoo pajamas.

ERMA [getting up]: Why, dear, what's the matter?

DAWN MARIE: I think she's scared or something.

ERMA: I told you, Fred, we shouldn't let the kids watch *Swamp Creatures of Death*. They'll all be having bad dreams. [Erma leaves the room, turns off the TV set]

DAWN MARIE: Daddy, you should have seen the man with the saw. He had this giant ten-tickle around his neck and his face was getting all blue and he was making this funny croaking sound and then he sawed off the ten-tickle right in time and this red stuff squirted all over the saw and . . .

FRED: Never mind, Dawn Marie.

DAWN MARIE: . . . And then he sawed off two more ten-tickles and then . . .

FRED: And then what happened?

DAWN MARIE: And then Sarey threw up, that's what!

ERMA [re-enters]: Well, I cleaned up the mess and turned off the TV set and put the slumber party to sleep. Fred, I read this book by Bill Betterman called *Protecting Your Child's Mind,* and it said that we shouldn't allow the children to view any kind of entertainment they can't handle emotionally. Did you know that the average child grows up seeing eleven thousand stabbings right on television?

FRED: Ah, Erm, I don't think it hurts to see a squid or two sawed up. It teaches them to be strong in the face of terror. It's kind of creative violence.

ERMA: You should have seen Sarey's pajamas, if you think that. I wouldn't be at all surprised if Dawn Marie has bad dreams. You know what else this book says?

FRED: Wanna finish the game or not?

ERMA: No, even though I'm winning.

FRED: Erm, if you quit now you allow me to win by forfeit.

ERMA: Even if I own Boardwalk and Park Place and three other monopolies?

FRED: Yep.

ERMA: Even if I have you penniless with no possibility of winning?

FRED: Yep, you lose, Erm; Monopoly Rule 341b.

ERMA: I don't think I have the stuff to go any further after seeing Sarey's pajamas.

FRED [folding the board and putting away the money]: Good, I win because of your forfeiture.

ERMA: Fred, I walked into the room when they still had three tentacles to go. If you knew how bad the movie was, why did you let them watch it?

FRED: I didn't think it would hurt. Erm, if you ever watched them make a movie you'd never let one of them terrify you again. I mean, that whole set was just miniaturized rubber tubing and catsup. It is so phony how they do the whole thing.

ERMA: Well, it convinced Sarey. Bill Betterman says we should protect our children's minds because what we see and read becomes ourselves.

FRED: Oh, I think that's overstating the case.

MILO [enters coming in from a date]: Hi, Mom.

ERMA: Milo, have you ever seen *Swamp Creatures of Death?*

MILO: Yeah, I caught it on a double feature with *Spaghetti Brains* on Halloween Horror night.

ERMA: Well, it was on TV tonight and Dawn Marie's whole slumber party was watching it.

MILO: Even the squid and chain saw?

ERMA: I'm afraid so.

MILO: I couldn't sleep for a week after that.

ERMA: See, Fred? I told you! Bill Betterman says we ought to see that our children are watching beautiful images and reading wholesome stories. Fred, do you know what Philippians 4:8 says?

FRED: Now you are beginning to sound like King Sizemore.

ERMA: I thought he was your best friend. You were just telling me back before my lucky ten that he said I should be submissive just like Jane! King is such a know-it-all. He never seems to run out of Scripture verses, does he? I'll bet he even has a verse for moving the pastor out of his house during a building program.

FRED: Oh, I don't know. You're being too hard on King.

ERMA: He'll find a Scripture even if it's buried deep in the heart of Leviticus.

FRED [Phone rings. Fred answers.]: Hello . . . Oh, hello, King! No, it's not too late to call. No, we weren't in bed yet. I just soundly defeated Erm at Monopoly. I wound up with everything. Colossal finish. . . . Boardwalk and Park Place and three other monopolies. The Agape Boat Bible Cruise? Well, if Gil Roller sponsors it, it must be good. . . . Sure I'll talk to Erm about it. . . . You want me to tell her what else? . . . You found the perfect Scripture for her? Okay, but I don't think it will help! Okay, good night. [hangs up] King found a Scripture that might help you go for the selling of the parsonage.

ERMA: What is it?

FRED: Leviticus 25:31.

ERMA: I knew it! Well, what does it say?

FRED: It says the houses of the priests, if they have no wall around them, may be sold in a jubilee year. [Erma looks askance and disgusted.] Well, Erm, you have to admit it has no wall around it.

# S c e n e IV

# Shooting Monkeys in Madagascar

[It is a comfortable evening at home and Fred has just settled onto the couch. The phone rings and Milo answers it.]

MILO [yelling from upstairs]: Dad, it's for you!

FRED [irritated]: All right, all right, Milo. I'll get it. Who is it?

MILO: Sounds like one of your friends.

FRED: I don't have any friends who get me up out of my easy chair after I've had my dinner. [picking up the phone] Hello. . . . Oh, hello, King! . . . Yes, I did enjoy our coffee time last night. . . . Yes, I have talked to Erma about what we were talking about. I don't think she is going to go for it. She thinks it's not fair to the pastor. I tried to tell her we love the pastor just as much as she does, but she says she will have no part of it and won't try to get it going among the women. . . . Erma really isn't much of a motivator, anyway. Besides, I have a feeling that most of the women won't go for selling the parsonage. . . . So even if it would force the pastor's hand, she's not going to do it. What really scares me, King, is that sometimes it seems like Erma may actually be buying into his one-sided philosophy of missions and world vision. . . . Yes, King, I know what the Bible says about managing my household, but my family doesn't read the Bible enough to know they are supposed to let me manage . . .

ERMA [bursting into the room]: Fred, I'm so excited about all the things God is doing in Madagascar. . . . Oh, I'm sorry. I didn't know you were on the phone. [whispering] Remember, I've got this late-night meeting at the church tonight and . . .

FRED: I'll see you, King. . . . Yeah, maybe golf on the weekend. . . . Yeah, bye for now. [hangs up phone] What's all the excitement? What's going on at this late hour in Madagascar?

ERMA: Well, I'm sorry, Fred. Luella couldn't come early so we all agreed to have a little late-night meeting of the World Awareness Committee and . . .

MILO [enters]: Mom, why do you have to be so religious? Why can't you stay home and watch soap operas like all the other mothers?

ERMA [ignoring Milo]: I'm off to church.

FRED: Say hello to Luella and the Madagascar Girls.

ERMA: Fred, must you be so flippant?

FRED: Erma, why all of a sudden do you have to take this Madagascar business so seriously? Do you have to be so aggressive about it? Wouldn't it be better if you just lived a good clean life in front of other people and helped make potato salad for funeral dinners or something?

ERMA: But Fred, that's the problem with the whole church. There are so many needs, and we all have to reach to the needy and those who don't know God. It's like Pastor Smith says . . .

FRED [interrupting]: What amazing insights does he have now?

ERMA: Who?

FRED: The pastor.

ERMA: Fred, it seems like all of a sudden you and King and your friends don't want the pastor around anymore. What's he done that's so contemptible? He simply feels that it isn't reasonable to care only about our local church and never quite give a thought to those who die without Christ in all other parts of the world. It all fits for me, Fred. We can't claim to love a God who cares only for wealthy suburbanites. If we truly cared about our town, we would also care about the whole world. There's no use taking a lamp to Madagascar that won't burn in America.

FRED: Is that our thought for the day, Erm? Maybe the lamp we need here at home is a nice gymnasium.

DAWN MARIE [enters as Fred is speaking]: And don't forget the Brunswick automatic pinsetting equipment, Daddy!

FRED [ignoring Dawn Marie]: Erma, you're becoming as lopsided as the pastor in all this overseas concern. You're always at missions meetings, and you constantly talk about God. I ask you, Do you have to talk about God all the time?

DAWN MARIE: Daddy, I heard you say something about God the day you were working on the car and the jack fell.

MILO: I don't think that's what Dad meant, Dawn Marie.

ERMA [ignoring the children]: Fred, are we really as concerned about our whole world—I mean, are you, Fred? As long as we've been going to church I don't think I've ever heard you mention God out loud.

MILO: I guess that's 'cause you weren't in the garage the day the jack fell, Mom!

ERMA [still ignoring Milo]: Not that you have to talk about God all the time to be a Christian. But there's more to this lifestyle than we have ever practiced in our home. I'm not chiding you, dear. It's just that somehow Pastor Smith is opening my world. I see so much further than I used to. I'm going to church tonight to try to find out some more direct way of helping people—wherever they live—to get to know Christ.

FRED: I don't know, Erm. You can turn people off if you get too holy. I mean, it makes you seem weird. Couldn't you just bake a casserole for old Miss Lakin or something?

ERMA: Well, I heard Alice Long say that serving Christ is really a matter of loving Christ. It's like a marriage proposal. There is a time when love has to get bold. Even if your fiancée knows that you love her, there will never be a marriage unless you get the courage to pop the question. Most people are too shy to bring the matter of Christ up. Fred [her voice growing dreamy and far away], you remember the night you proposed to me?

FRED: Yeah, Erma. I felt great when you said yes.

MILO: Oh, brother . . .

ERMA: Well, the point is you changed my life, Fred.

MILO: And all for the worse too.

ERMA [ignoring Milo]: And yet I never considered your question too direct or offensive. I wanted you to ask the question because I realized my whole life would be better just because you asked it. I wanted to be your wife.

MILO: Why, Mom?

ERMA: Because I thought your father was just about the neatest person I had ever met.

MILO: Didn't get out much in those days, huh?

FRED: Okay, Milo. Cool it! Well, Erm, I guess there are times in life when direct questions are necessary. [momentarily sentimental] I can still remember how I popped the question: I said, "Erma, my dearest love . . ."

MILO: Oh, yick!

ERMA: Well, what if you had not been direct and asked the question? I never would have known for sure if you loved me or not. You had to ask so I could really tell. Love always speaks despite its fears: it's bold enough to . . .

FRED [shaking himself back into character]: But I don't see how this relates to people in Madagascar or your overblown concern! ERMA: Honey, the pastor says that real love is always direct. It's always bold. When there are people in great need, we must get involved and help because they're special to God. The pastor says that anyone can help and should . . . FRED: Pastor, Schmastor! Erma, I've heard all about that man I want to hear. You need to remember you're trying to learn from someone who doesn't care enough about our immediate world to give it a bowling center. How can Smith get so wrapped up in these holier-than-thou ideas and look past the bowling needs of his own church? ERMA: Still, a missionary is a missionary. I think it's kind of thrilling to be right here and yet be one with others in Madagascar. FRED: Maybe. Maybe, Erma. Have you done any more praying about the parsonage? Leviticus 25:31. Remember it doesn't have a wall. It could be sold! ERMA: Fred, I looked that verse up. It doesn't seem to say at all what King thinks it says. I don't think King is above bending the Bible to make a point. Anyway, I'm off to church. Would you mind helping Dawn Marie say her prayers and tucking her in for the night? Thanks, you're a dear! [She gives Fred a peck on the cheek, grabs her coat and runs out the door.] FRED [calling out after Erma]: Okay, honey! Dawn Marie, it's time for you to be in bed! Did you pray for all of the missionaries? DAWN MARIE: Yes, I always do, Daddy, because Pastor Smith says that we should always pray for all of the missionaries. Daddy, do natives in foreign lands like to bowl? FRED: I dunno, Dawn Marie. What makes you ask such a question? DAWN MARIE: I just wondered. I know you don't like to see the poor people in the jungles have bowling alleys like we do. FRED: Now, Dawn Marie, that's not true. Every native tribe should have the right to bowl if they want to. Daddy just wants to be sure that we have bowling alleys here before they do. If we give all our money to them and they buy food with it, then nobody will have one. Besides, natives can't find bowling shoes just everywhere, and missionaries are too busy to bowl.

DAWN MARIE: Daddy, what do missionaries do all day?

FRED: Well, they get up early, sweetheart, and tiptoe through the jungle shooting monkeys till they find a native, and then they tell him to get some clothes on if he wants to become a Christian.

DAWN MARIE: And do they do it?

FRED: Sometimes they do and sometimes they don't.

DAWN MARIE: My Sunday-school teacher said that she prays for a missionary in Lagos and that they have buses and airports just like we do.

FRED: Oh, I don't think so, honey! They don't even have frozen dinners or baseball cards!

DAWN MARIE: Oh, then they must be very poor.

FRED: Yes, you can't have hardly any money or they won't let you live in Africa. If they had much money, they would want Adidas and Corvettes, and it's hard to want to be a Christian once you get a Corvette. Missionaries are poor too. They only get one camera and enough money to buy film so they can take pictures of monkeys and sunsets.

DAWN MARIE: Daddy, are there lots of snakes in the jungles?

FRED: Of course, and no missionary can even be ordained until he wrestles a twenty-five-foot anaconda and pins him three times. If you can get one skinned it's all the better because you have something to hang over the piano in American churches on missionary night. One time the Whiteheads of Swaziland had leather coats they had made from wildebeests and iguana belts made from iguanas they had found in their beds right after they said their prayers. That's why missionaries pray so much; it helps keep the iguanas over in the natives' beds.

DAWN MARIE: My teacher says that many natives suffer from malnuition.

FRED: *Mal-nutrition,* Dawn Marie.

DAWN MARIE: It makes their arms bony.

FRED: Yes, it's caused by severe hunger over a period of time, sweetheart.

DAWN MARIE: My teacher says that we should all give money to help feed the poor people.

FRED: Well, I guess so, Dawn Marie.

DAWN MARIE: Daddy, could we give a little money to help feed the poor?

FRED: I dunno about money. We have to eat ourselves. We'll just pray that all the natives will stay in the jungles and have nice monkey sandwiches like God intended, honey.

DAWN MARIE: My teacher says that in many parts of Africa they don't have jungles anymore.

FRED: That's silly, honey, of course they have jungles. All of Africa is one big jungle full of plump monkeys—four drumsticks on each one!

DAWN MARIE: My teacher says that Africans have cut down too many trees to build cooking fires and now they don't even have parks and no food at all. Everything is desert, and everybody's hungry and needs us to send money so they can all have little dishes of rice and wheat. They don't even have any wild animals they can eat.

FRED: Oh, honey, I don't think that's true. Where would the Whiteheads get their jackets?

DAWN MARIE: My teacher thinks we should all skip one meal a week and send the money we save to Chad.

FRED: Then the Chadonians will have all the Burger Doodles and Discount Cities and we'll all go hungry.

DAWN MARIE: We could all go to the zoo and make monkey sandwiches, Daddy!

FRED: Dawn Marie, be realistic.

DAWN MARIE: Daddy, could we make a family pledge to missions? My teacher says we can all make a pledge because we are rich compared to other people of the world.

FRED: Rich! Dawn Marie, we eat at the Burger Doodle three nights a week now just to save money. I wouldn't call that rich.

DAWN MARIE: My teacher says . . .

FRED: Your teacher has obviously got more money than most of us!

DAWN MARIE: I don't think so, Daddy. She's handicapped.

FRED: Handicapped?

DAWN MARIE: She has to walk with a cane, Daddy, and she cleans houses for a living. But she still says we can share with those who are less fortunate. Are we less fortunate than my teacher, Daddy?

FRED: Go to sleep, Dawn Marie. . . . I'll see you at breakfast.

DAWN MARIE: I'll see you in the morning, Daddy.

[Lights dim momentarily and then come on again as Erma returns from her church meeting. Fred is found sleeping in his chair with TV on but no program being broadcast.]

ERMA: Fred, are you asleep?

FRED: No, not now. What time is it?

ERMA: Oh . . . not too late. Fred, is it true there are no trees in parts of Africa?

FRED: Of course it's not true. You've seen all those Tarzan movies. He lives in the trees.

ERMA: Yes, but Luella says that the people have cut down all the trees and now they are starving. Fred, I was wondering whether or not we might not make a bigger pledge to . . .

FRED: I dunno, Erm. Charity begins at home, you know. If we keep sending money to the Africans, they'll be eating just like Episcopalians, and you know where we'll be?

ERMA: At the Burger Doodle?

# ACT III

# Scene I

# The
# Mongeese Men

[Three months have passed since the fateful board meeting where Pastor Smith met with King, Stu, Harry and Fred. The MacArthurs have just finished dinner and Fred is preparing to go to his lodge meeting just after he finishes watching Gil Roller on television. Fred belongs to Lair #73 of Royal Men of the Mongoose.]

FRED: Honey, look what I got in the mail today; a new book by Gil Roller. *Top of the Ladder, Top of the World!* I found out that Gil Roller made over ten million dollars last year—not bad for a preacher. He has a cross-shaped swimming pool and a church with Brunswick automatic pinsetting equipment.

ERMA: Does he make all that money off his television ministry?

FRED: No, Erm. He just preaches on Sunday and the rest of the week he's one of the new directors of LifeDream, a company that sells quality kitchenwares and fine furnishings. His church held the original True Man Seminar.

ERMA: True Man Seminar?

FRED [ignoring Erma]: I've been looking at a way to get some more income. Stu Johnston says that we're an embarrassment to God when we don't succeed in life. That's why I signed up for the True Man Seminar this weekend. I can hardly wait. True men who are true to God always seem to have a good income. Know what I think? I think it's because God blesses them. I wish Pastor Smith would preach just like Gil Roller. Smith is so boring! Always concerned about the missionaries in other parts of the world. Erma, here and now is where it's at. He needs to get where it's at. Christ came to bring us abundance—John 10:10.

ERMA: Oh, Fred, you're quoting Scripture.

FRED: Yes, but I didn't learn it from Pastor Smith. He never quotes the good ones. Erm, I learned this one from Gil Roller. I'm going to quote it for King Sizemore the next time I see him.

ERMA: Fred, here's your turban! Want a cup of coffee while you watch Roller?

FRED [slipping into his turban]: I guess so. I'll barely have time to watch Roller tonight! I need to get to lodge early. We're initiating a new pride tonight.

ERMA: Really? That's nice. What's a pride?

FRED: You know, quail come in coveys, chickens in flocks, mongeese in prides.

ERMA: I thought lions came in prides.

FRED: Well, for some reason, so do mongeese.

ERMA: I see you're wearing another new suit.

FRED: Well, nothing is too good for the Mongeese, Erm.

ERMA: I still keep hearing what Pastor Smith said about people who put all their money into clubs and lodges and give so little time or money to Christ.

FRED: Well, Erm, I don't want to hear any more about Smith. I think that gray suit he wears is a disgrace, an embarrassment to the whole congregation. He couldn't get into the Mongeese dressing the way he does.

ERMA: Still, it seems there's a lot of fire in his preaching lately. It's like he's a trapped man, living in cultural abundance and carrying a tremendous burden for the world. It's plain unreasonable, Fred! Is he growing more and more distant from the rest of us?

FRED: I don't want to hear about him.

DAWN MARIE: Daddy, what's a mongoose?

FRED: Well, Dawn Marie, a mongoose is a small ferretlike animal that is respected in Asia because it kills cobras.

DAWN MARIE: Gosh, Daddy, can you kill a cobra?

MILO: Actually, most Royal Mongeese just drink a lot and sponsor carnivals.

FRED: Button up, Milo! No, Dawn Marie, the Royal Men of the Mongoose are a benevolent and humanitarian society which is dedicated to truth and compassion and altruism in the pursuit of a better world.

MILO [begins drumming with his hands on the table top and singing to the tune of "Battle Hymn of the Republic"]:

Glory, glory for the Mongoose.

Keep your vodka mixed with orange juice.

If you're not afraid of cobras, you can live it up till dawn.

The Mongoose marches on . . .

ERMA [pleading]: Milo, don't upset your father. You know how he loves his lodge.

FRED: I do love it, Erm, and we Mongeese do a lot of good . . . for God and country.

MILO: Besides, you have a football pot and Friday-night poker.

FRED: We are a spiritual organization. We quote Scripture and all of our steps to Mongoosehood are founded in the Bible. I remember many years ago when I was just being initiated as a Mongoslin, I had to learn many verses. I've forgotten most of them now.

DAWN MARIE: Daddy, what's a Mongoslin?

FRED: Well, a Mongoslin is a little Mongoose. Like little humans are called children, little Mongeese are called Mongoslins. Every one of our great Mongeese was once a Mongoslin.

ERMA: Who were some of them, Fred?

FRED: Well, Erm, all through history Mongeese have served God and their fellow man.

MILO [begins drumming and singing again]:
   Genghis Khan and Machiavelli,
   Hitler and Machine Gun Kelly . . .

FRED [ignoring Milo]: Well, there was George Washington's chaplain.

ERMA: I didn't know that he was a Mongeese!

FRED: Mongoose.

ERMA: Mongoose. What was his name?

FRED: Reverend Mordecai Liberty.

MILO: Dad, isn't Mr. Bell the barber . . .

FRED: Why yes, Milo. How did you know?

MILO: Well, he has beady eyes like a Mongeese.

FRED: Mongoose.

MILO: Mongoose. And the haircuts he gives you look like he could have been in pet-trimming once.

DAWN MARIE: Mary Eddistein thinks Mr. Bell is retarded 'cause he picks his nose right in front of the glass in his barber shop.

MILO: All the Mongooses do it.

ERMA: Do you remember how you worked day and night memorizing the Anticobra Code of Fangs and Life?

FRED: Well, yes, Erma . . . [begins repeating the code aloud] It shall be my duty as a lover of Mongoose Law to strive to see above the density of tyranny . . .

MILO [drumming on the table, sings]:

Glory, glory, Dr. Seuss,

Fred MacArthur is a Mongoose.

ERMA [ignoring Milo]: Well, Fred, you worked so hard on that code. You stayed up for nights . . .

FRED: I believe in being dedicated to what's worthwhile.

ERMA: But remember when the pastor asked you to teach a children's Sunday-school class? You said you were just too busy and couldn't work it into your schedule.

FRED: Well . . . I . . . I . . . I wanted to, Erm, but . . .

DAWN MARIE: Daddy, how come you'll study Mongooses and not teach Sunday school? My teacher said Jesus loved the children and . . .

MILO: Yeah, but Jesus wasn't a Mongeese, Dawn Marie. Was he, Dad?

FRED: Well, Milo. We don't know for sure. But we think that there was a Royal Lodge in Nazareth near the middle of the first century and maybe . . .

ERMA: *Stop it, Fred!* I won't have you telling the children Jesus was a Mongoose!

FRED [becoming embarrassed]: Well, Erm, we don't know for sure . . .

DAWN MARIE: He couldn't have been, Daddy, 'cause he never sinned!

MILO: *Wow!* That's true, Dawn Marie.

FRED [Phone rings. Fred answers.]: Hello . . . oh, . . . hello, Pastor. No, I can't. . . . Yes, I'd love to teach the eighth-grade boys but. . . . I just couldn't work it into my schedule now. . . . That's all right. . . . Thanks for thinking of me. . . . Yes, good-bye, Pastor. [Fred hangs up.] Know what he wanted, Erm? He wanted me to teach a Sunday-school class. What does he think I am, anyway? Eighth graders! It's like Roller says, "Limited success men have limited vision!" Eighth graders! I ask you!

ERMA: Well, Fred, somebody has to teach them. Do you think Gil Roller could possibly be wrong?

FRED: Why, Erma? What could possibly be wrong with preaching Jesus and getting rich?

ERMA: I don't know, but Gil seems richer than Jesus was. Jesus was a poor carpenter who taught renouncing your wealth and taking up your cross.

FRED: Now Erma, you stop that negative talk right now. Gil Roller says you need a Mighty Mental Mindset, and *your* MMM is masochistic. You actually enjoy being poor, don't you, Erm? You're beginning to sound like Smith. . . . By the way, have you noticed that he is still wearing that same gray suit every week? Has for over three months.

ERMA: Madge says that she heard that the pastor has given away all his clothes and only has that one suit.

FRED: That's why he'll never be a successful pastor. Gil Roller would call that a crummy one-suit attitude toward life. Speaking of Roller, Erma, it's seven o'clock now! It's time for "The Hour of Heart and Hope!" [Fred hurries to the set, turns on TV and switches the UHF selector to something in the high seventies. The voice of Gil Roller immediately fills the room.]

GIL ROLLER: . . . That's why tonight I am preaching on "Rock and Roll: The Devil's Footwork." Many of you young people have given your lives to the godless pursuit of rock and roll when it's been proven time and time again that rock and roll was developed by the Communist Party in 1936 to bring about the dissolution of all freedom-loving people in the West. It is a shame unto God for good Christian young people to dance and have fellowship with the entire scene of drugs and drums.

FRED: Amen!

GIL ROLLER: You don't have to listen very long to this godless music to realize that rock and roll is a return to the jungle.

FRED: Amen! Amen! Are you listening, Milo?

GIL ROLLER: Furthermore, it has been proven that the blatant tempo of savage sound and filthy-dirty modern rock and roll lyrics loosens the sexual controls, and many fallen young women attribute the beginning of their fall to rock and roll.

FRED: Amen! Amen! Are you listening, Milo?

GIL ROLLER: Oh, my brothers and sisters, time would not suffice for me to tell you of how often broken young women and once handsome men have come to me with their arms full of the impressions of needles and terrible drugs that all started on the floor of the dance hall where they were playing that godless rock and roll music. Sometimes, even while they dance, you can hear the amphetamines, like the teeth of sneering demons, jiggling in the pill bottles in their too-tight jeans. It's time to stand up! Let's turn from the filthy-dirty modern rock and roll that is destroying our world and poisoning the minds and hearts of our youth.

FRED: Amen! *Amen!* AMEN! Milo . . . MILO . . . wake up . . .

MILO [coming alive out of a drowsy trance]: Oh, I wasn't asleep, Dad.

FRED: Milo, this is a brilliant man. Everything he is saying is true. Besides, he is a spiritual man!

MILO: You can tell by the sheen on his cowboy boots, Dad, that he is pure as Tex Twang and the Tumbleweeds.

GIL ROLLER: In my last crusade thirty-two glue sniffers came down the aisle and put their tubes on the altar. They turned from the sin of sniffing and gave up their vices. But every one of the thirty-two derelicts said they had first sniffed on the floor of a rock and roll concert. Mothers and dads, never let your kids go to another rock concert as long as you live!

And now we are going to stand and sing hymn #452 while hundreds of you make your way down the aisles. Come and get your crummy morality straightened out. While hundreds of you are making decisions all across this great land, we'd like to remind each and every one of you watching at home that you can have a part in the Gil Roller People's Steeple . . .

MILO: Dad, it's all over. Mind if I turn it off?

FRED: I guess not, Milo. Did you hear what Roller said about rock and roll and the death of Western culture?

MILO: Dad, do you think it's possible that we hear in sermons only what applies to other people? You know who I admire as much as anyone?

FRED: No, Milo.

MILO: Pastor Smith.

FRED: Smith? Why Smith? Have you listened to Gil Roller's tapes or read his books? Why your mother and I are even planning on going on one of his Bible cruises. Milo, Roller can help you too. He can make a success of your young life.

MILO: Dad, it's just that when I listen to Gil Roller, I have the feeling that he never cries. And when I listen to Pastor Smith, it seems like his whole life is a cry . . . from the heart. Dad, I think he really means it when he says that the world needs Christians who know how to care and who are willing to take up their crosses and follow Christ.

FRED: When did he say that?

MILO: At communion last week when he challenged us to give up the amount of money we would spend on food in one week and give it to the world hunger offering. Know what I did? I have been saving my lunch money and doing without lunch so that I could give.

FRED: You mean, you haven't eaten all week, Milo?

MILO: Aren't you proud of me, Dad?

FRED: Proud! Milo, I give you lunch money so you can eat. You better eat!

MILO: *But Dad!* Don't you see what would happen if everyone would share a little? Pastor Smith is right. Every little baby that starves to death was a baby that God loves as much as he loves Dawn Marie. He has to love everyone the same or he wouldn't be much of a God. Remember when Pastor Smith said that Jesus once took a boy's lunch and shared it with a multitude of people? Our world cannot go far without the example of what Christians do in the face of great need.

FRED [after a long period of silence]: Cat got your tongue, Son?

MILO: Dad, does Gil Roller really have a cross-shaped swimming pool?

FRED: I've gotta go to lodge, Son. . . . Bye.

MILO: Say hello to all the mongooses!

FRED: Mongeese.

# Scene II

# Why Does God Hit People with Beer Trucks?

[Erma is ironing. Fred is reading the paper. The doorbell rings several times. Reluctantly, Erma puts down the iron, adjusting the heat indicator to off, and goes to the door.]

ERMA: Oh, hi, Madge. Come on in.

MADGE: Hi, Erma. I can only stay a minute. I was just driving by and thought I'd stop and give you the latest for the prayer chain.

ERMA: Well, I'm glad you did.

MADGE: Listen, Erm, it's the Harris boy.

ERMA: What's wrong with the Harris boy?

MADGE: He was driving his folks' car late last night and was hit head on by a beer truck.

ERMA: Oh, that's awful. Will he live?

MADGE: I'm afraid so . . . I mean, yes, but he will have to be in the hospital for a few days, so I wanted to ask you to pray for him. They say Billie Lou is terribly upset about her son's accident, but you know Billie Lou—there's not an ounce of spirituality in that woman! As neurotic as she is, I'm sure the good Lord must wonder how she keeps up her religious front in the church. There she is—teaching a class on the victorious Christian life and hitting the Valium just to clear up her shakes so she'll look like she is filled with the peace of Christ. If you ask me, the Harris boy wouldn't be such a juvenile delinquent if Billie Lou weren't such a phony. I've heard it from a couple of very reliable folk that the Harris boy smokes a lid of grass a week. And some say that he pops his mother's pills between puffs.

ERMA: Well, I certainly will pray for him.

MADGE: Have you ever taken Billie Lou's class on the victorious life?

ERMA: No, but I could use it—I've been a bit depressed lately.

MADGE: Listen, you take Billie Lou's class and you'll be a weeping vegetable. I've got this friend who says that when she took three of the sessions, she felt so bad that she considered quitting the church. If you ask me, Billie Lou's negative Christianity is driving some good people away. No wonder the Harris boy stays out all night popping pills and smoking grass. It's our Christian duty, I suppose, to pray for him. Billie Lou's "victorious life" forced her wild kid right into the radiator of a beer truck.

ERMA: Have they tried to get counseling?

MADGE: Who? For Billie Lou or her son? Lord knows they both need it. I'll be honest with you, Erm, I don't know how much good it does to pray for people like the Harrises. I always feel like I'm just pouring a lot of rich spirituality down the drain. It's just like it says in the Bible, "God helps them that help themselves."

ERMA: Where does it say that?

MADGE: I think I could pray a little harder for Billie Lou Harris if she worked a little harder at being worthy of my prayers. As for her wild-eyed son, I hope she sees the hand of God in this. I mean, if my son was living on grass and rock concerts, I'd consider it a direct sign from God if he was hit head on by a beer truck.

ERMA: Well, Madge, how is Etta Louise?

MADGE: She's just fine—that sweet little three-year-old of mine—I'm sure never gonna raise Etta Louise so that God has to hit her with a beer truck to teach her his high and lofty ways.

ERMA: You say it was head on?

MADGE: Head on!

ERMA: But he's okay?

MADGE: If you call a ruptured spleen and a broken leg okay.

ERMA: But he is going to live?

MADGE: He'll be on crutches, I'll wager you. He'll be on crutches till he learns the sweet lessons of God.

ERMA: About how long will that take, Madge?

MADGE: Can't say for sure—but I hope he does. I hope this whole incident will teach the Harrises that they better live a little more like Harvey and I do. Well, I gotta go . . .

ERMA: Well, thanks for stopping by.

MADGE: Don't forget to pray for the Harrises and call the next person on the prayer chain and ask them to pass on the request, okay?

ERMA: Okay. Bye, Madge.

MADGE: Bye! [exit]

FRED: Goodness, Erma. Listening to Madge makes me wonder if that prayer chain isn't more like a gossip circuit.

ERMA: Well, Madge said Mike Harris is nothing but a drug addict. [enter Milo] Where have you been, Milo?

MILO: I went by the Harrises'. Did you hear what happened?

FRED: Yes. Mom got all the dope from the prayer chain. You keep away from Mike, Milo. He's drugging and boozing. You gotta be bad to get hit by a beer truck.

MILO: He's never been into drugs. Maybe sometime you could call the prayer chain and set 'em straight. I shoveled the Harrises' driveway. Mike won't be able to do it for a while. I wish I had some money, Dad. Mrs. Harris couldn't afford insurance. Fortunately, she thinks the beer company will settle up okay. But in the meantime, things are a little tough. Mike Harris works at a service station to help out. Well, I'm going to get started on my homework. [exit Milo]

FRED: Erma, why does God hit people with beer trucks?

ERMA: Maybe he didn't, Fred. Maybe it was an accident. Maybe it becomes an opportunity for all of us to be a little more like Milo.

FRED: Erma, do you think Pastor Smith is getting to Milo?

ERMA: Maybe Pastor Smith. Maybe it's God. But whoever it is, there's something good about it.

FRED: I have the feeling I don't know anybody around here anymore. I hope he doesn't turn out to be the same kind of weirdo as Smith. I don't think I could handle it, Erm! I hope King and Stu force the issue soon on the Christian Life Center . . . for Milo's sake, we need to get a new pastor.

# S c e n e III

# Milo's Date

[Fred and Erma are waiting for Milo to arrive and introduce his date for the evening. Although Milo has dated Kim a few times, Fred and Erma have never met her.]

FRED [obviously angry]: I just don't see why the boy can't date one of our kind.

ERMA: I think Kim is our kind, and she is a nice girl!

FRED: That's not the point, Erma. Nice is one thing. Chinese is another.

ERMA: Well, my family is all Lithuanian, and yours is British.

FRED: Yes, but our colors are the same.

ERMA: Ah, Fred, are you prejudiced?

FRED: Certainly not! I bought a cup of coffee from Willie Wang over at the computer center—cost me forty-three cents too. Now does that sound like a prejudiced man? I own a Toyota car with a Sanyo stereo in it too. Chinese is fine in cars and stereos, but Milo . . .

ERMA: Has gone too far, right? Besides, Toyota and Sanyos and Kim are all Japanese, Fred.

FRED: Don't get technical, Erma. Chinese, Japanese—not a nickel's worth of difference between the two . . .

ERMA: Well, Kim is a fine girl. Oh, look, here they come now. Now be nice, Fred. [Kim and Milo enter.] Hello, kids. How are you doing? Come on in.

MILO: Mom, Dad, I'd like you to meet Kim.

FRED and ERMA [stand and greet Kim]: Good to meet you.

[Milo shows Kim to a seat beside him on the couch. Fred shifts in his chair and looks a little uncomfortable. He begins the conversation.]

FRED: Well, Erma, it certainly is nice to have Kim in our home, isn't it?

ERMA: It *is* nice to have you, Kim.

KIM: Thank you, Mrs. MacArthur.

ERMA: Oh, you can call me Erma.

FRED: And you can call me Fred.

MILO: And you can call me Milo.

KIM: Thank you.

FRED: You speak very well—I mean, good English.

KIM: I was born in Los Angeles; so were my parents and grandparents.

ERMA: Isn't that nice, Fred? Her family has lived in America longer than yours. Fred's parents were immigrants.

FRED [shifting uncomfortably again]: Yes . . . well . . . uh . . . Erma, why don't you fix a big pot of green tea and we'll all put on thongs and eat fortune cookies. Ha, ha . . . uh . . .

KIM: No, thanks, I just had a bowl of chili at the Nacho Sombrero and a bunch of us are going out for pizza after the game.

FRED: You eat chili and pizza?

MILO: Oh, come on, Dad! Kim eats normal nutritious food like hamburgers and candy bars.

FRED: Your father runs a restaurant on the east side?

KIM: No, my father . . .

FRED: Runs a laundry?

KIM: No, actually, my father . . .

FRED: A rickshaw in San Francisco?

MILO: Please, Dad, Kim's father is vice president at the bank.

FRED: Which one?

KIM: First National.

FRED: That's our bank!

KIM: He's in lending and escrow, so if you ever need to borrow any money . . .

FRED: Kim, we're so proud of you, and we sure hope that you and Milo have a good time at the game. Want a bag of Oreos from the Orient? Get it? Ha . . . uh . . . well . . . [Milo and Kim stand to leave, and Fred and Erma follow them to the door.] It's been nice to meet you.

ERMA: Have a good time, kids. [Fred and Erma take a chair across from each other.]

FRED: Well, you know Asians aren't as yellow as I always thought.

ERMA: It's amazing how being in charge of loans makes you almost as white as if you were a British immigrant.

FRED: Now, Erm, I don't like that tone in your voice.

ERMA: What if Kim's parents had run a little laundry or owned a little Cantonese place called The Golden Chopsticks? But if her dad's in the chips, you can overlook the color barrier. Right, Fred?

DAWN MARIE [enters singing]:
Jesus loves the little children,
All the little children of the world.
Red and yellow, black and white,

They are precious in his sight.

Jesus loves the little children of the world.

Mommy, was Jesus from Asia?

ERMA: Well, he lived in the Middle East, so I guess so . . .

FRED: Now wait just a cotton-pickin' minute! I don't mind saying God loves all colors, but Jesus was not Chinese.

ERMA: Well, he wasn't British either, Fred.

FRED [changing the subject]: Who would have thought they'd eat chili and pizza? Probably do it with a fork too.

ERMA: They probably use very nice forks! He's a bank vice president!

FRED: Bank vice president . . . a man like that could be useful to me, Erma. I sure hope Milo doesn't do anything to offend Kim. Maybe if they get on well, I'll stop by the bank and have a chat with her dad. I've been thinking about trying to get a little home improvement loan and . . .

ERMA: Maybe we ought to stick to our own kind, Fred . . . I think there's one more thing you ought to know about Kim.

FRED: She drinks saki? You know I won't have that, Erma.

ERMA: No, Fred. She's a missionary volunteer.

FRED: She's going to become a missionary? How did she get all tangled up with Milo?

ERMA: There's probably one other thing you ought to know.

FRED: This thing is getting pretty tangled . . . oh, no . . . Don't tell me Milo is going to be a missionary.

ERMA: Well, not exactly; but you know he's been going to that Bible study Pastor Smith has been having. They are studying *The Principles of Christian Loving.* It's a great book, Fred, especially for those who are considering missions as a lifetime career.

FRED: Surely you can't be talking about Milo.

ERMA: I don't think so, Fred. But you have to admit there have been some tremendous changes in the boy in the last few months, and who can tell what in the world he's been thinking all this time?

FRED: If Pastor Smith talks my son into going to Madagascar there will be hell to pay. He could have a great football career with the Bushwackers and get rich and famous, just like God intended him to be.

ERMA: Ever hear of a man named C. T. Studd, Fred?

FRED: No, but I like the name. It sounds macho.

ERMA: Well, he was in a way. He was a famous athlete in England at the end of the nineteenth century. He made a lot of money as a famous cricketer, but he gave up his fame and reputation and career to become a missionary.

FRED: What in the world made him do a stupid thing like that?

ERMA: Those who knew him said he was driven by a strange, inner compulsion that only found rest when he thought that he was pleasing God.

FRED: You don't think that Milo and this Asian girl are getting those kinds of ideas, do you, Erma?

ERMA: I don't know, but it doesn't seem to me that they are not all that interested in bowling centers anymore, Fred. Maybe they think there's something more important.

FRED [whispering]: Erm, something is happening to Milo. For one thing, he's losing his good judgment. He likes the pastor better than Gil Roller. He's got to be sick, Erm. Stu and King told me that they are going after the pastor now. They'd like to see him resign and replace him with somebody more progressive.

ERMA: What makes them think it's their place, Fred?

FRED: Well, I don't know, Erm, but I see their point. We've got to turn this church around. I think that's what's the matter with Milo. Who ever heard of a young, red-blooded American male who would rather be a missionary than play football?

DAWN MARIE: Daddy, Milo's got seven dollars in his little world bank.

FRED: Oh, no! Not again! Erma, speak to him. He's not eating his lunch at school. He'll be anorexic if he doesn't stop this non-sense.

ERMA: I don't think so, honey. He eats twice as much as ever at evening meals. . . . He'll be okay. I think Milo is thinking over a lot of things now, dear. I saw him reading his Bible after school the other night.

FRED: Why would he do that when I've given him so many neat books and tapes by Gil Roller?

# Scene IV

## The True Man Seminar

[Fred is seated in the back row of the class. He is wearing a designer shirt open to midchest with an overlarge, pseudomacho gold chain around his neck. He is holding a note pad in his lap along with a copy of *The True Man,* a new best seller by Biff Beefington. Beefington, one-time Hollywood stuntman, lately born again, has just entered the room and begun to speak. Fred, having been on a diet after reading chapter four of *The True Man,* is a little out of sorts and has just had a major tiff with Erma before leaving for the Holiday Haven Hotel ballroom where three thousand are gathered for the seminar. Seated by Fred is King Sizemore who, in addition to *The True Man* and note pad, has in his lap a seventeen-pound Bible, well-thumbed and worn.]

BIFF BEEFINGTON: Good evening, gentlemen. Welcome to The

True Man Seminar. It's great to see all three thousand of you out there. In the next two days I'm going to help you discover that to be truly godly is to be truly manly. Here and there throughout my presentations I want to show you film clips from movies I have made. I thought I was a real he-man before. But believe you me, I only discovered true manhood when I discovered Jesus, and he was a man's man, and there has never been a true man who didn't think so.

Well, let's pray: God, we thank you we are men—true men. Help us this weekend to discover that *macho* is not a dirty word, nor is *tough.* Help us to realize that when things get tough in life the tough get going. Help us to remember that your Son called himself the Son of *Man* and he also called himself the *true,* and Father, help us to remember that if we put those two Scriptures together, we can see that Jesus was a True Man, even if he never read my book. In the name of truth and manhood. Amen.

TWO THOUSAND VOICES: Amen!

BIFF: What was that?

TWO THOUSAND FIVE HUNDRED VOICES: Amen!

BIFF: What? Let's hear a real he-man's amen! AMEN?

THREE THOUSAND VOICES: *AAAAA-MEN!*

BIFF: That's better now. Never forget that a True Man isn't ashamed to say *amen. Amen?*

THREE THOUSAND VOICES: *Amen.*

BIFF: What was that?

THREE THOUSAND VOICES: *AAAAA-MEN!*

BIFF: That's better. Remember in this conference we will be saying A-*MEN* and not Awomen, and we will be singing *hymns,* not *hers.* [laughter] Maybe you heard about the preacher that was preaching against bossy wives and said, as he thumped the pulpit, "Just remember this. There are no perfect men in this world. Do any of you know a perfect man?"

A little thin man raised his hand and interrupted the preacher and said, "Yes, sir, I do!"

"Who is it?" thundered the preacher.

And the little wimp said, "My wife's first husband." [laughter from the crowd]

Well, there was only one perfect man. And, oh, that man was a True Man. He came down from heaven and they hung him on a cross and he died for Biff Beefington. [stops and wipes a tear from his eye] Yes, my friend, a True Man cries about the right things. He doesn't cry about soap operas, and if any of you men are watching those godless soap operas, you ought to get down and ask God to forgive you. They call them Daytime Dramas now, but they are soap operas. They only call them that because every writer and producer ought to have their minds scrubbed out with soap. Amen?

ONE THOUSAND VOICES: Amen!

BIFF: What did you say? Sounds like we have some wimpy little soap opera watchers . . . What did you say?

THREE THOUSAND VOICES: *AAAAA-MEN!*

BIFF: Now remember this, men: tears are not a sign of weakness. I want to show you a film clip of a three-hundred-foot drop I made in flames. I was in an asbestos suit covered with sterno. I was ignited and then dropped one hundred and eighty-seven feet before I deployed my chute. . . . Are we ready with the film clip? [The lights dim and the projector comes on, illuminating a big screen behind Beefington.]

FRED [whispering underneath the Dolby sound system]: King, is this guy for real?

KING [whispering back]: Of course, Fred. Tim Dithers used to be a real wimp before he took the True Man Seminar. Now he's in charge in life. He just bought a Ford Bronco, and now he baits his own hooks in the Bass-o-Rama down at Finger Lake. He handles his missis in good shape too! He keeps her in her place. I think the course would have helped that wimp, Adrian Flowers, but his wife kept taking Biff's book away from him.

FRED: I dunno, I don't think I would ever want to "handle" Erma. She's so sweet!

KING: Don't go soft, Fred. A man should rule his own house. . . . Wow, look at that film!

FRED: Wow! I don't know if this guy's macho or nutso!

[Film clip stops. Thunderous applause breaks into the air as the lights come up.]

BIFF: Ah, men, that was a thrill. But I'll tell you, it cannot compare to the thrill of knowing Jesus. Yes, one day I was out on my Harley just ridin' nowhere. I was thinking of killing myself. I was lower than a snake's belly! I decided I was gonna shoot up on coke and just ride that Harley off El Capitan and write Biff Beefington out of the script of life. Then just ahead of me I saw a truck—a sixteen-wheeler with ICHTHUS on his mud flaps, and across the back of his trailer there was a fluorescent sign that said, "Truckin' for Jesus!" Well, I followed him to the next truck stop, and he pulled off and I pulled off right behind him. I thought since he had that Jesus stuff all over his truck, he'd be a little pink shrimp of a man. But he was macho . . . big as a Hell's Angel . . . and I sat down by him at the truck stop, and he stuck a chaw o' Skoal in his lip and opened up the Word and I saw Jesus. [begins to cry again] Yes, Brothers, he was towering a million miles high. This wasn't any little shrimp of a Savior, this was El Shaddai Jesus. A Savior with ten-penny nails in his hands and heavyweight macho. And I just fell at his feet and he forgave me. And I went and got on my Harley and I didn't shoot up with coke and I didn't drive off El Capitan. I drove back to Paramount Studios and I did this scene from *Kodiak!*

[Lights dim. Projector comes on.]

FRED: Wow! Look at the size of that bear. He must be ten feet. And look at Beefington going after him. This guy really is a True Man! Tim Dithers ever hunt big game after this seminar?

KING: No, but he drove a dune buggy across the Mojave last summer, and he landed a spoonbill underneath the spillway. Never goes anywhere without his copy of *The True Man* either.

FRED: Does he read the Bible much?

KING: Says he can't understand the Bible with all those big names and the begats, so he just reads *The True Man*. Adrian's wife took his copy away from him and beat him up with it 'cause he wouldn't mow the lawn. Adrian just takes it, Fred. Adrian told his missis that he allowed that he would buy him a Harley and follow Christ just like Biff. Know what his missis said?

FRED [distracted by Biff's struggle with the Kodiak]: Uh, uh!

KING: She asked him if they made Harleys with training wheels. . . . He just stood there a minute; then he cheeped and went to bed. Know what I think I'm gonna buy, Fred? A jeep and a thirty-ought-six rifle . . .

[The lights begin to come up as the film clip dies to thunderous applause.]

BIFF: Now men, you don't have to confront a Kodiak to prove you're a True Man—although it helps—but you do have to be in charge of life. Now Jesus don't sponsor no wimps! The True Man runs his home and his factory, and yet he submits to the Macho Messiah who hung out there on a hardwood cross and begged God to forgive the sissy wimps that put him there. He was the True Man. Amen?

THREE THOUSAND VOICES: *AAAAA-MEN!*

BIFF: Well, let's all take a little break . . . Everybody stand and take a manly stretch . . . We'll reconvene in fifteen minutes.

FRED [standing up quietly, stretches and grabs his coat]: See ya, King!

KING: Where ya going, Fred?

FRED: I'm going home to Erma; I've got to apologize. I treated her so rotten tonight.

KING: What are you, Fred, a wimp? You gotta be more macho.

Biff is going to tell all of us that no woman will love a man she can't respect. You can't show weakness—that's why our whole culture is in trouble. Amen?

FRED: See ya, King!

KING: C'mon, Fred, stick around. After the intermission Biff is going to show us a clip from *Terror in the High Sierras.*

FRED: I don't know, King . . . It all seems like a lot of hype and . . . Hi, Stu . . .

STU [walking briskly]: Where you going, Fred?

KING: Fred had a little tiff with Erma, now he's all out of sorts. He thinks he needs to go home and apologize.

STU: Apologize? What is this, Fred? Who wears the pants in your family anyway?

[Fred ducks his head and doesn't answer.]

KING: Fred, did you or did you not talk to Erma about the parsonage thing?

FRED: Several times now, but she's soft on Smith. . . . I don't think she's going to help.

STU: She's going to have to do it. Our wives aren't as central in the swim of the church as Erma.

FRED: Well, she says, "No go!" She thinks the pastor has enough problems right now.

STU: He doesn't have any more than he's created. Hi, Harry!

HARRY [walks up and shakes hands with the other three]: Hi, Stu! Great conference, huh? Did any of you hear Gil Roller's sermon on Ezekiel 37? He says that in the last days there will be false prophets that have a form of godliness but deny the power of it. That's Smith's problem. He's always talking about God, but he just never gets anything done for God right here in this community.

STU: Harry and I have been talking, and we think that we've come up with a way to turn things around. Harry is going to make a motion at board meeting that we suspend all giving to missions until we resolve what's best for our community. I'm going to make a motion at the end of the meeting that we put the whole issue of the Christian Life Center back on the table.

FRED: Stu, that won't help. I tell you, too many people in the church agree with him. Erma thinks we need to be more concerned about the world around us, and Milo, who's always been loud and critical of everything, seems to be going through some kind of change.

KING: What kind of change?

FRED: I don't know. He's reading his Bible all the time, and he even said that he felt that Pastor Smith was leading the church in the right way.

KING: The right way! The man's down to one suit and gives most of his money away, and now he wants us to send our hard-earned bucks to Madagascar.

FRED: Still, Stu's motion is not going to work. There are too many people who agree with the pastor, at least right now. I think we ought to cool the whole issue and call it off.

STU: You're wrong, Fred. They will listen.

FRED [growing red in anger]: You're wrong, Stu. They will not listen.

STU: Now cool down, Fred, and I'll tell you why they will listen. You know that little inheritance that I received? Well, Blondie and I wanted to do a little something special for the Lord 'cause he's done so much for us. We thought of giving the money to the church, but we know that Smith would just funnel it on through to Madagascar, and we'd be buying monkey sandwiches for everybody on the island. Well, we decided we'd give the whole thing to the church, but designate it all to the Christian Life Center so that not one dime of it could get into Smith's pet projects . . . if you know what I mean.

KING: The whole thing? But that was half a million dollars, wasn't it, Stu?

STU: Six hundred thousand, to be exact.

KING: Wow, that's some kind of money. . . . Are you sure you wouldn't like to send a little to the Gil Roller Evangelism Ministries?

STU: No, we've thought it through, and we believe that our sweet and precious Lord wants us to give it to our local church, but he wants it to stay local too.

FRED: Amen . . . *amen* . . . *AMEN!* Maybe you're right, Stu. Maybe the church would listen to us after all.

STU: I think they will, and we'll put a stipulation on it, Fred. The church can have the money if they not only build the Christian Life Center but put in those . . .

KING AND FRED: Automatic Brunswick pinsetters! Yahoo!

STU: Of course it will take another million or two to complete the project, but we'll have the whole project on the board, and maybe the church will be able to think of a way to come up with the rest of the money.

FRED: I know how Erma and I can help. . . . We'll make a motion to sell the parsonage and give the money that we make off the old place to the Christian Life Center.

KING: And if Smith doesn't like the arrangement, maybe he'll just be that much more interested in moving on.

HARRY: Hey, did any of you guys catch Gil Roller last night on television?

ALL: Nope.

HARRY: He's going to build a big retirement center near Visalia. Three hundred and twenty-five million simolias!

[The others gasp.]

All for Jesus too. And he is building a twelve-hundred-foot spire . . . one hundred feet for each of the apostles.

KING: What a man of God!

HARRY: He's gonna call it the People's Steeple, towering over Rollerville, his new Condo-for-Christ village. Know what his God-will-provide text is? "Give, and it shall be given unto you . . . pressed down, and shaken together, and running over"—Luke 6:38.

FRED: Isn't Visalia right on top of the San Andreas fault?

HARRY: Yes, but three years ago Gil prayed for God to heal the San Andreas fault, and they haven't had a tremor since. Besides, the foundation for the People's Steeple will be built out of concrete laced with little bags of sand they're bringing from the Holy Land. Isn't it marvelous?

FRED: It's wonderful, but won't you and Lettie be giving your money for the Brunswick automatic pinsetters right here in our hometown?

HARRY: Yes, of course, Fred. . . . Now don't get defensive, but we believe that what we send to Gil Roller God will give back to us pressed down, shaken together and running over, don't you? Then when God gives it all back to us, we might even buy you a new bowling ball with "Try God" etched on it, Fred.

FRED: Aw, thanks, Harry. . . . Well, has everybody got down everything that we are going to do at the board meeting next week?

KING: I'm set!

STU: Me too.

HARRY: "Pressed down, and shaken together, and running over." *. . . Count me in and give me some skin!*

[all slap hands]

KING: Hey, I'm starting a little Bible study group next week. We're going to be studying Biff Beefington's book, *The True Man.* You guys in?

STU: Count me in!

HARRY: "Pressed down, and shaken together, and running over."

FRED: Well, I don't know . . . I . . .

STU: Well, King, why don't we all study Roller's book *Ladder to the Top of Babel?* I have a friend who said it's the best one-volume work on succeeding in the last days so you don't have to be raptured penniless.

KING:  Could you go for it, Fred?

FRED:  Sure, King!

KING:  Could you, Harry?

ALL:  "Pressed down, and shaken together, and running over." . . . *Count me in and give me some skin!*

# ACT IV

# S c e n e I

# Breezy Willows
# and
# Summer Butterflies

[The MacArthurs are at Dawn Marie's piano recital. Fred and Erma, speaking in stage whispers, are on the back row. The room is crowded and the air conditioning isn't working.]

MRS. STRINGENDO: And now Samuel Hammond . . .

FRED: What number is Samuel Hammond, Erm? How come Milo didn't come?

ERMA: Thirty-three, Fred. Shh! I'll tell you later.

MRS. STRINGENDO [continuing from the front of the recital room]: . . . will play Mozart's Minuet in G. Many of you may not be aware of it, but Mozart was from Salzburg, Austria.

FRED: How nice! She probably isn't aware of it, Erm, but Willie Nelson is from Nashville. Why can't you tell me where Milo is?

ERMA: Shh, Fred . . . I can . . . later.

MRS. STRINGENDO: . . . Samuel is one of our best pupils and says someday he'd like to visit Austria. Samuel's grandmother is here all the way from New England to hear him play. [limited applause] Samuel, tell everybody what Mozart's other names were.

SAMUEL [beaming]: Wolfgang Amadeus.

FRED: Good grief. . . . Play it, Sam, for heaven's sake!

MAN FROM THREE ROWS AHEAD [turning toward the MacArthurs in the back row]: Shhh! [Samuel begins to play.]

FRED: Erm, whaddaya think the score is in the Bushwackers' game? What number is this kid?

ERMA: Thirty-three. I told you, Fred.

FRED: Erm, there's only four more till Dawn Marie. . . . Isn't this exciting. Erma, don't any of these little piano bangers know "Blue Eyes Cryin' in the Rain"? I don't think Sammy Hammond has hit one note right, has he? Erm, can you see? Is that kid wearing mittens?

ERMA: Fred, it's about over.

[Samuel Hammond quits, stands and takes a bow, after which there is limited applause and Mrs. Stringendo stands up and begins introducing the next student.]

FRED: What number is this one, Erma? Erma, if Milo winds up in Madagascar with Luella Colby's ugly sister. . . . Erma, promise me you'll try to get him to read one of Gil Roller's books before he does something internationally reckless!

ERMA: Thirty-four, Fred. . . . What do you mean, . . . reckless?

MAN IN FRONT: Shh—quiet, please.

ERMA: We'll talk about it later, Fred.

FRED: Oh, oh. This kid is big. He'll probably play one of those thirty-minute jobs.

MRS. STRINGENDO: Now Jacob Willman will play the entire Sonatina 32 by Muzio Clementi.

FRED: Oh, good, one of my favorites. What luck, the whole thing!

MRS. STRINGENDO: I know if each of you listen, you will be able to catch the contrapuntal spirit of the piece. [She sits down and Jacob begins to play.]

FRED: Erm, did I ever tell you of the time I caught the contrapuntal spirit? I was in bed for three weeks! I think I feel it coming on again. Erm, what is Dawn Marie playing?

ERMA: She's playing "Breezy Willows and Summer Butterflies."

FRED: You mean, I'm sitting here risking my health to contrapuntal spirit and waiting on "Breezy Willows and Summer Butterflies"?

FAT MAN IN THE SECOND ROW [turning toward the MacArthurs]: Shh!

[Fred grows quiet for the remainder of the concert. The lights dim momentarily and then come up again on the MacArthur family in the car on the way home from the recital. Fred turns up the volume on the last five minutes of the Bushwackers' game.]

FRED [listening to the radio]: Behind! Erm, they're behind. While I was listening to "Breezy Willows and Summer Butterflies," my team was in pain.

DAWN MARIE [begins to cry]: Mommy, why didn't Daddy like my piano recital?

ERMA: Oh, he didn't just like it, honey! . . . he loved it!

FRED: I did not. I hated it. I can't believe I've got the only complete collection of Tammy Wynette in my motor pool, and I'm listening to Wolfgang and all those medieval composers. [Fred gets quiet and listens to the radio a minute.] Oh, my gosh, Erm, they're gonna let the rookie from Wyoming attempt a field goal at thirty yards!

DAWN MARIE [crying]: I don't feel good, Mommy.

ERMA: Well, honey, the recital room was too hot.

FRED: Yeah, and all those sweaty little Mozarts were reeking with the contrapuntals, you could tell. You probably picked it up off the keyboard after that Hammond boy. I'll bet he had the allegretto too.

DAWN MARIE: Mommy, could we stop the car?

FRED: Stop the car? Here in the third lane of I-423? Not on your life! See, I told you. The rookie missed the field goal. That's what happens when you take a bowlegged cowboy and try to teach him to kick . . .

ERMA: Fred, I think you better stop . . .

FRED: Oh, all right, Erma. [Fred works his way to the outside lane and Dawn Marie gets out on the shoulder side of the freeway.] Poor little thing! Erm, I'll tell you . . . she's got the contrapuntal for sure. Those piano recitals can ruin your health. Ever notice how Waylon Jennings and all the great musicians play guitars and drive pickups? You don't catch them retching by the side of the road.

[Dawn Marie is soon back in the car and the MacArthurs are back in the traffic, headed for home.]

DAWN MARIE: Momma, did *you* like "Breezy Willows and Summer Butterflies"?

ERMA: They were beautiful and you played it beautifully.

DAWN MARIE: Momma, I don't think Daddy liked my recital. . . . Mommy, does Daddy love me?

FRED: Great Scott! They fumbled on the forty . . . *fumbled on the forty* . . . [pounds the dash] *FUMBLED ON THE FORTY!*

ERMA: What's the worst possible fumble you can make in this game?

FRED: Hmm . . . I guess if you fumble the ball deep in enemy territory . . . like on the one-yard line.

ERMA: You didn't hear the recital tonight.

FRED: What do you mean? I heard every one of the thirty-nine pieces. And I even learned things that I didn't want to about Amadeus.

ERMA: You still want to know why Milo wasn't at the concert?

FRED: I just assumed he was at the track, running.

ERMA: Wrong again, quarterback. He was at the life-encounter rally. I think we're losing Milo. He's . . . losing interest in football and . . .

FRED: And what . . . ?

ERMA: Fred, we could be losing Milo. We may be about to fumble on the one-yard line.

[Fred switches off the radio and all sit in silence as the car hurries on.]

# Scene II

# What King James Begat

[Fred and Erma are in a bookstore to select a new Bible.]

FRED [to salesperson]: Excuse me, sir. I was looking for a Bible. I've got plans to attend King Sizemore's new spiritual life Bible study, but my eyes are just not what they used to be. I need to find an understandable Bible I can read.

CLERK: I'll be glad to help you! Did you want something basic or a Bible with more study helps? We have our Larson Living Links Reference Bible with annotated Psalms.

FRED: Well, I don't know. I guess so. . . . It's like King says, "The Word of God is a lamp unto my feet." . . . okay . . . how much is it?

CLERK: It's on sale this week for only $80.00.

FRED: $80.00—that's a pretty expensive lamp, young man! How

much is it with plain ol' Psalms and no references?

CLERK: Maybe you would like to see the Buddy Study Bible with the classified concordance and the color-coded center strip.

FRED: Is it readable? I mean, no "thees, thous or begats."

CLERK: Yes, sir. We have it in modern English, the MRV with the new MRV concordance.

FRED: Gosh, it sounds like a ballistic missile! How much is it?

CLERK: Well, in this maroon leather binding with India paper it's $59.95.

FRED: The Indians must charge a lot for their paper now. I don't think I want to support those Hindus. How do you like that, Erm. We send all these Bibles overseas, and they charge us for the paper. How much is this same Bible printed on good old American paper?

CLERK: I'm not sure if we have one printed on "good old American paper," sir.

FRED: No wonder the balance of trade deficit is out of sight. . . . I told you, Erm, we should have just taken the Bible out of the Lake Ponchetrain Motel last summer.

ERMA: Fred! He didn't mean that!

CLERK [smiling but unsure]: Sir, would you like a cheap Bible that's easy to understand?

FRED: I sure would!

CLERK: Then we have the Vivacious Version—easy to understand.

FRED: How much is it?

CLERK: $9.95.

FRED: Wrap it up. No, wait a minute. Would you mind reading me the twenty-third psalm?

CLERK [uncertainly]: Well . . . all right. [turning pages; stops] "Because the Lord of life is really my fantastic shepherd . . ."

FRED: Why does it start "because"? It should just start out, "The Lord is my shepherd."

ERMA: Please, Fred!

CLERK: ". . . I have all the goodies of life waiting for me . . ."

FRED: Does that mean, "I shall not want"?

CLERK: I think so, sir! [continues reading] "He lets me lounge about in verdant grass . . ."

FRED: What is this? A Bible for dairy farmers? Does that mean, "He maketh me to lie down in green pastures"?

CLERK: I think so, sir! [continues reading] "He helps put the zip in the zipper of life, even when I'm sick."

FRED: Sounds like Medicare—it's supposed to say, "He restoreth my soul," isn't it?

CLERK: It still says that in the old King James.

FRED: That must have been the one my mama read to me when I was a child.

CLERK: Yes, sir. [continues reading] "He makes me leap to my feet to serve him. Even when . . ."

FRED: I don't like this cheap economy Bible! Erma, they over-printed on this one. It doesn't even sound like the Bible. Give me one of those old King James. I'm sure they cost a lot more, but I want a Bible that sounds like *the* Bible.

CLERK: Well, I'll be glad to do that, sir, but just remember—it's gonna be full of thees and thous and begats. You might not understand it.

FRED: Oh, I don't know—I wasn't at the top of my class, but I did pretty well with *Julius Caesar* in the eleventh grade.

CLERK: Very well, sir, here is a copy of the old King James. That'll be $14.95.

FRED: Not so fast. Read me a little bit of it so I can be sure.

CLERK [opening the Bible and reading]: "In the beginning God created the heavens and the earth."

FRED: Not that passage. The twenty-third psalm.

CLERK [opening toward the middle of the Bible]: "The Lord is my shepherd; I shall not want."

FRED: Now that's more like it, sonny. That's how the Bible is supposed to sound.

CLERK: Yeah! Well, how about this one, sir: "And Arphaxad begat Salah; and Salah begat Eber. And unto Eber were born two sons: the name of one was Peleg; for in his days was the earth divided; and his brother's name was Joktan. And Joktan begat Almodad, and Sheleph, and . . ."

FRED: Ah, that sounds like the true word my mother used to read to me.

ERMA: But Fred, do you understand?

FRED: I understand that this is a real $14.95 Bible and not a $9.95 Medicare manual.

ERMA: But honey, I think you ought to buy a Bible you can understand.

FRED: I want the *true* Bible. If it was good enough for Mama and Granmama and the apostle Paul, I don't think we ought to replace it with one of the $9.95 wonders. Erma, I'm surprised at you wanting to replace the true Word of God. It's just like Gil Roller says. People are going soft on the true Word. . . . It's a sign of the end of time.

CLERK: Will that be cash or check or credit card, sir?

FRED: Credit card! Sonny, do you know that the day is coming when credit cards will be the mark of the beast? They're going to take those numbers off those cards and put them on your forehead with invisible ink that only shows up when the antichrist comes by and shines a little light on you. Remember what Gil Roller said? "Give up your credit cards before they build the temple in Jerusalem." Are they building that temple yet? Do you know?

CLERK: I don't think so, sir.

FRED: Then I guess it's all right to make one last charge on the old plate. But if you ask me, sonny, I wouldn't put none of those $9.95 Bibles on a credit slip 'cause if the rapture comes you could be left with a lot of credit slips and a box of phony Bibles.

CLERK: I'll remember that, sir. Here's your Bible and happy reading.

FRED: Erma, what does *begat* really mean?

ERMA: In one of those $9.95 Bibles it says it means "fathered."

FRED: Well, it might mean that, but you know, Erma, in Bibles you get what you pay for. I guess if the true Word says that Arphaxad begat Salah . . . well, we will just have to take the Bible at its word.

ERMA: I guess so, dear!

FRED: Young man . . .

CLERK: Yes.

FRED: Would you happen to have a copy of *Ladder to the Top of Babel* in the store?

CLERK: Gil Roller's new book on how to succeed in the last days?

FRED: Yes.

CLERK: I sure do! Here! It's $17.95.

FRED: $17.95! That's more than I just paid for the Holy Bible.

ERMA: Well, Fred, do you want to succeed in the last days or not?

FRED: Well, I guess so. I need a copy for the Bible study. . . . Okay, young man, I'll take it!

ERMA: $17.95—at this much per copy I guess Gil Roller will be succeeding in the last days.

CLERK: Excuse me, sir, but I couldn't help but notice your name on the card—you're not by any chance Milo's father?

FRED: Well, yes . . . yes, as a matter of fact, I am.

CLERK: He's a good friend. He was just in and picked up a biography of C. T. Studd I ordered for him a month ago.

FRED: Studd? The macho missionary?

CLERK: Mr. MacArthur, some of us were wondering why Milo always wears that same pair of jeans with the gray pullover sweater.

# Scene III

# The Agape Boat Bible Cruise

[Fred and Erma stand looking out over the back railing at the wake of the S. S. Marguerite, a Royal Dane Luxury Liner.]

FRED: Erm, I feel awful on this boat. Why did we come on this Agape Boat Bible Cruise anyway?

ERMA: It was your idea, Fred. You were the one that sent in for that Gil Roller brochure for the Bahamas cruise.

FRED: Well, I still feel awful.

ERMA: I know, Fred, but at least we didn't have to leave until the church board meeting was over and the whole issue of the new Christian Life Center was settled.

FRED: It was sure great to see the new spirit of togetherness after Stu and Blondie announced their generous gift.

ERMA: It was generous. Still, I felt sorry for the pastor. . . . He seemed so . . . beaten. . . . It was as though he had failed to turn the church to see the needs of the world. It was like he was a . . . a . . . a surgeon who had lost his patient on the operating table.

FRED: Erm, I think you're being melodramatic. [shrugging his shoulders and changing the subject] How long have we had this cruise planned?

ERMA: About three months, Fred.

FRED: I'm so sick! I can't believe I've been waiting this long to feel this bad. Everything looks green.

ERMA: You're kind of cute when you're green, Fred.

FRED: Erm, any more Dramamine?

ERMA: It's back in the cabin, Fred. I'll go get you some. I hate to see you so nauseated and irritable.

FRED [irritably]: I am nauseated, but I am *not* irritable!

ERMA: I'm sorry, dear, I didn't mean to imply anything. You remember what our textbook is: Zelpha Zippinger's *No Sickness, No Hard Times, Just Jesus!* Gil Roller wrote the introduction.

FRED: If this ship doesn't stop wobbling, I think I'll throw up.

ERMA: The tide is high, Fred. . . . Zelpha says that all sickness comes from faithlessness, and that if we really trust God, we'll never even have a headache again.

FRED: I know I'm going to throw up. You read too many wacko books, Erm. Maybe you ought to try to cut back on that kind of stuff. There was a lady back in Boynton Falls that went crazy because of reading too many God books. She finally thought she was a faith healer, but she died before she could really get her ministry off the ground. It always seems funny when a faith healer dies . . . and they all do sooner or later, Erm.

ERMA: Zelpha Zippinger died last week too.

FRED: Hmm! *No Sickness, No Hard Times, Just Dead!*

ERMA: Fred, I'm sorry you've been so seasick on this cruise. I just wanted you to enjoy the Bahamas and Brother Willis's lectures on the disciplined life and the Mighty Mental Mindset.

FRED: He's fifty pounds heavier than I am. Erm, how can the man teach us anything on the disciplined life? And did you see him at the ship's dessert bar?

ERMA: I'll bet you wouldn't be complaining if it were Gil Roller instead of his associate lecturing on success. Oh, look, Fred. There's a sea gull . . . and it looks like there's gonna be a moon tonight. Isn't it romantic?

FRED: I think I'm gonna throw up!

ERMA [taking Fred's arm]: Come on, honey, let's go see what Harriet and Harold are doing. I'll bet they're with Brother Willis at the dessert bar right now!

FRED [starting to go with Erma]: I'm sure I'm gonna throw up! [catching sight of Willis Willoughby] Hi, Will!

ERMA [quickly under her breath]: Dr. Willoughby, Fred; where's your respect?

WILLIS: You lovebirds been up watching the tide? [He quickly shoves a petit eclair into his mouth.]

ERMA: Fred isn't feeling well, Dr. Willoughby.

WILLIS: Not feeling well? You do look a little green around the gills, Fred.

FRED: Seasickness, I guess, Will . . . er . . . Dr. Willoughby.

WILLIS: Nonsense, my boy! No such thing! Have you been reading our text for the cruise—*No Sickness, No Hard Times, Just Jesus* by Zelpha Zippinger?

FRED: Isn't that the late Zelpha Zippinger, Dr. Willoughby?

WILLIS: Well, . . . yes, the late Zelpha Zippinger . . .

FRED: Who died of pneumonia after a Whole Mind, Whole Body, Whole Destiny Conference?

WILLIS: Well, yes . . .

FRED: The same Zelpha Zippinger who wrote the song:
In heaven there's no sickness and when heaven gets in you,
You can't have a common cold or the Asiatic flu.

In heaven there's no cancer, lumbago or arthritis.
No angel in the court of God ever had nephritis.
No saint on Glory's golden streets ever had bursitis.
So brother when we walk by faith, Satan cannot spite us.
Just walk by faith and you will have no sickness or hard times
'Cause Jesus will delight us.

WILLIS: Well, yes . . .

FRED: I think I'm gonna throw up!

ERMA: Maybe we shouldn't have gotten one of those inside state-rooms next to the diesel engines, Fred. Dr. Willoughby's room has two portholes.

WILLIS: Three . . . one for the Father, one for the Son and . . .

FRED [reaching for his sick sack]: Nice little peephole on the world while you eat cream puffs and write lectures on the disciplined life, huh, Will?

ERMA: Fred . . . that didn't sound very kind. Dr. Willoughby is a man of God and he is very disciplined.

WILLIS: It's okay, Erma. [taking a sip of a cup of coffee and eating the last bite of a raspberry torte] Fred isn't feeling well. [Willis turns to walk away, but calls back over his shoulder as he leaves] Fred, I'll tell you, I haven't been sick a day in my life since I started walking by faith. [begins singing] In heaven there's no sickness and when heaven gets in you . . .

FRED: Erm, was Zelpha Zippinger disciplined?

ERMA: I have no idea, Fred . . . I suspect so . . .

FRED: I mean, was she fat?

ERMA: Her picture on the back of the book looks like she was a little overweight, dear. Why do you ask?

FRED: Erm, what are we doing on Disciplined Life Cruises eating cream puffs and reading books by Zelpha Zippinger, anyway?

ERMA: Fred, you're not feeling well. . . . It's that cheap stateroom by the deisel engines that's making you sick. I told you we should have gotten an outer room with a porthole.

FRED: Look, Erm, it's this whole cruise that's making me sick. Don't blame it on the cheap room. I fished with Harold and Bill in a wallowing tug for two weeks and never got sick. I think Willoughby and a rough sea are too much for me. I just don't trust a thick lecturer on Christian discipline.

ERMA: He's Gil Roller's right-hand man!

FRED: I wish it were Gil himself. Anyway, Erm, I've had enough. I'm going back to my little room by the diesel engines. How many more days, Erma?

ERMA: Day after tomorrow we'll be home! Home . . . I wonder how the whole Christian Life Center is coming along? I talked to Blondie, and she says they are really getting the rush at church since they announced their gift to the building program . . . six hundred thousand—that's some gift. Everybody appreciates it.

FRED: I'll say everybody appreciates it, and the way they designated it, it can only be used for the Christian Life Center.

ERMA: And they've made a stipulation that it must have the Brunswick pinsetting machines, too. It must have made you very proud, Fred. . . . Still, I feel sorry for the pastor.

FRED: Whatever for?

ERMA: Well, Fred, the parsonage thing! The apartments of this city are so expensive and condominiums are out of sight. Somehow the board's action seems a little cruel.

FRED: Cruel! Erma, I haven't seen this much excitement around the church in years.

ERMA: Well, it is exciting, but haven't you sensed a great deal of fatigue in the pastor lately?

FRED: Maybe Pastor Smith just never really did have a knack for getting ahead in the world. I ought to lend him a copy of *Ladder to the Top of Babel.* Maybe it would help him invest his salary a little better and get ahead more.

ERMA: Maybe the church should pay him a little better and he'd have more to invest.

FRED: Erma, he would have more to invest if he would quit sending so much to Madagascar. I don't feel a bit sorry for him. Erma, this is the twentieth century—the day is gone when you can succeed just by going to church and sending money to missions. I think Pastor Smith needed to learn years ago that God didn't mean for us to give away all of our resources and then mooch off the hard-working church member who pays the bills in Madagascar. The man needs more of a sense of discipline . . . it's all in the third chapter of Gil Roller's new book. You can't lay around and ever hope to succeed in life . . . I'm sure it's been a bitter lesson for the pastor to learn. . . . Anyway, "tears are the divine cleansers of old vision," at least, that's what Gil Roller says.

ERMA: What do you think Milo will do with his life? He seems to feel Pastor Smith lives out the sacrifice so many Christians just talk about. He put a lot of his old clothes in the Madagascar missions crate.

FRED: Whatever for?

ERMA: He said he had way too many and couldn't wear them all in a year . . . and if they could be of use to someone somewhere, maybe . . .

FRED: Erma, we've got to stop Milo. He'll be down to one suit too. Stop him, Erm—he'll listen to you!

ERMA: I'll talk to him when we get home.

# Interlude

MILO: The parsonage sold today. Pastor Smith is looking for a new apartment in the city. He'll feel at home there. A lot of people feel he's going to resign. Like I said, Tranquility Community Church has never been happy anyway! I don't know if I see things exactly as they are, but I try to be honest about the poor of Madagascar or the down-and-outers downtown.

Wanting more is universal, I'm afraid. I've begun to see so many things: we are Christians and Christians should never accept life just as it is. We can share and we should. At least *I can and I will!* One thing for sure I've learned from Pastor Smith: right is something you do without looking over your shoulder to see if anyone else is doing it too. Sometimes it's a solo flight all the way. We MacArthurs are about to have a special caller and I want to be home when he gets there, or at least before he leaves.

# Scene IV

# Jesus
# Waxahatchie

[Fred and Erma are seated in the living room going through mail.]

FRED: I can't believe all this mail piled up while we were gone on the cruise. Here's the church newsletter. Look at this, Erma. We're going to send $5,000 more to Madagascar. . . . This ugly lady is going to get it. . . . Her picture is right here.

ERMA: Who? Let me see. . . . That's Luella Colby's sister, Fred. She's not ugly.

FRED: Well, she sure looks like it. . . . She looks like she's been on monkey meat and fried bananas.

ERMA: Fred, stop it! I won't have you talking that way.

FRED: Look, it says, "Milo MacArthur challenges youth to 'skip lunch and feed a bunch.' Milo MacArthur told forty high-schoolers that merely by skipping lunch on Wednesdays, the youth of the church . . ." [Fred interrupts himself.] Why can't Milo get off this kick?

ERMA: I don't know, . . . but I'm so proud! [opening the mail] Oh, Fred, here's a letter from Aunt Hattie in Waxahatchie!

FRED: What's the old bat . . . er . . . uh . . . What's Auntie doing, Erma?

ERMA: She's real excited. [Erma begins reading.] "Dear Erma and Children, . . . "

FRED: She never forgets me, does she, Erma?

ERMA: Well, Fred, . . . she's old. [continues reading] ". . . I know that you must be doing well. I am so excited. I was made the Methodist representative on the Jesus Waxahatchie Committee.

FRED: Is Jesus going to Waxahatchie?

ERMA [ignoring Fred, continues reading]: ". . . it is all such an honor. We are going to have the meeting in the high-school stadium on the Fourth of July weekend. We are having a gospel quartet, a Christian jogger, a converted communist who rowed his junk to freedom from Haiphong Harbor . . ."

FRED: You don't row a junk, Erm. The man's a phony.

ERMA: "We tried to get an associate evangelist from Indianapolis named Hal Hotspur but were unable."

FRED: Who does he associate with in Indianapolis?

ERMA: Biff Beefington?

FRED: Not a chance, Erma. I know all those guys . . .

ERMA: Personally?

FRED: You know what I mean . . . their names—and there's no Hal Hotspur in the B. B. Association.

ERMA [continuing to read]: ". . . Each night after the main meeting there is going to be a Moonlight Crusade with a different concert artist. At Jesus Amarillo they had more than three thousand decisions . . ."

FRED: That many!

ERMA: "Of course, we are not expecting so many decisions here in Waxahatchie, but our steering committee is trying to get the Gospel Royals to sing. They're all Methodists but real solid . . . in fact, the bishop said they are one group whose theology never gets in the way of their old-fashioned dedication to Jesus . . . "

FRED [interrupting]: What about the fireworks at the county fairgrounds? Aunt Hattie has always sold ice cream there for the Daughters of Texas.

ERMA: Fred, how thoughtful of you to remember. [continues reading] ". . . I know I have always served ice cream at the county fairgrounds for the Daughters of Texas, but I had to ask myself, after sixty-eight years as a Methodist pillar, which is more important—the Daughters of Texas or Jesus Waxahatchie? And of course, Erma, you know who won. Besides, there's something so showy about the fireworks at the fairgrounds, and I guess the Daughters of Texas will just have to do without me this year. When I think how our Lord turned from the showy to the service of others, I'm exceptionally proud to be a part of Jesus Waxahatchie.

Now let me tell you about the main services at the stadium— first the song leader is going to do a concert under the lights singing songs from his latest album, *Penthouse Hymns*! And then the converted hooker is going to share her testimony: 'Men I knew before I came to the Man of Galilee!' And then the Greater Waxahatchie All-Church Choir is going to sing . . ."

FRED: Maybe Aunt Hattie won't miss the fireworks all that much.

ERMA [continues reading]: ". . . then, if we get the Gospel Royals at the Moonlight Crusade, we should have hundreds of decisions . . . especially if they sing selections from their new album *Hot Grace*! I just love their song,

I'm higher than I've ever been before
Since I heard him knocking at my door
No more drugs and no more booze

Puttin' up my dancin' shoes
Since I heard him knocking at my door.
It's a wonderful song. I'll send you and your husband a cassette."
FRED: My name's Fred, Aunt Hattie!
ERMA: "They're organizing a huge prayer campaign, but I don't think I'll get involved in that. I think prayer is important, but I just can't do everything, and the committee has asked me to make a churn of ice cream for the crusade staff after the services on the fourth. I may make some of my fresh peach ice cream. A couple of the Daughters of Texas are mad at me for skipping the exercises at the fairgrounds, but what I'm doing is far more important and far less worldly.

"Well, Erma, I guess I'd better go. Three of the girls are coming over for a book study on the deeper life. I thought I'd stir up a batch of those Nashville Nuggets—everybody loves those cookies. Don't forget to pray for Jesus Waxahatchie. By the way, our main speaker is going to be Gil Roller. Have you ever heard of him? Some fellow with a big church in California! Give my regards to Milo and Dawn Marie and your husband."
FRED: My name's Fred, Aunt Hattie! Gil Roller, did she say?
ERMA: Gil Roller—wouldn't King Sizemore like to be there? Well, she's a stout heart, but so dedicated. I just can't believe that she would sacrifice the Daughters of Texas for Jesus Waxahatchie, can you?
FRED: Here's five dollars, Erm.
ERMA: Five dollars! For Jesus Waxahatchie?
FRED: No, Erm. Send it to the Daughters of Texas.
ERMA: Oh, look, Fred, here's a letter from the church board. They must have had an emergency meeting while we were gone.
FRED [almost grabbing the letter and tearing it out of Erma's hands. Fred reads.]: Well, if that don't beat all. Stu and Harry and King, three of our most powerful board members, are calling for the pastor's resignation.

ERMA: Oh, no! Fred, he's getting along in years. He may not be able to get another church.

FRED: Maybe something will open up in Madagascar.

ERMA: Oh, Fred . . . I feel so bad about this.

FRED: It had to happen, Erma. The church has to join the twentieth century.

ERMA: Maybe . . . maybe the congregation will vote to keep him on. All of us on the missions committee, I am sure, will vote for him.

FRED: Erma, you wouldn't!

ERMA: Fred, I can't stand by and let a fine man be hurt like this.

FRED: Fine man! Erma, he didn't even want to have the Brunswick bowling center. How can you call him a fine man? Stu's the fine man . . . he's six hundred thousand worth of fine, and maybe now his gift will allow our church to really reach out as it should. With a new pastor this could become a real Gil Roller kind of church. [Erma buries her face in the church letter and Fred suddenly looks shocked as though he has only really understood for the first time. The doorbell rings and Fred walks to the door and is stunned to find Pastor Smith.] Pastor Smith . . . uh . . . won't you come in? Erma, honey, it's the pastor!

ERMA [shocked]: Pastor Smith! Come in. I'm so glad to see you! I wish Milo were home. He thinks so much of you. He would be so glad to see you . . . not that Fred isn't . . .

FRED: Oh, yes, uh . . . yes . . . we're so glad you've called. Won't you come in? Here, have this chair.

ERMA: Tea? . . . Yes? . . . I'll fix some and be right back! [Erma hurries from the room.]

PASTOR: How are you, Fred?

FRED: Fine, Pastor. But how are you?

PASTOR: We're doing splendidly, thank you. I thought you might like to know that the parsonage sold today. The buyers want to take possession of it toward the end of next month.

FRED: Well, I'm glad . . . I mean, I'm sorry . . . I mean, I'm glad the old place sold and you won't have to live there anymore and we can use the money for the new Christian Life Center . . . but of course I'm sorry that you'll be having to move now. Any idea where?

PASTOR: Not quite yet, but I'm sure we'll do all right somehow. . . . I came for another reason, Fred. You know Erma has been very regular in meeting with our overseas missions committee, and I wanted you to know, as well as her, that I'm planning to leave Tranquility Community.

FRED: Quit?

PASTOR: Yes . . . well . . . resign, Fred, after a great deal of thought and much prayer.

FRED: Just like that?

PASTOR: Well, it is not at all as abrupt as it seems.

FRED: I suppose not, but it does seem abrupt.

PASTOR: I've been thinking and praying long and hard about the future of the church. It seems that with the new building plans underway, it will not be long until we will be breaking ground for the new Christian Life Center.

FRED: Thanks to Stu and Blondie's generous gift . . . should be a nice facility.

PASTOR: Yes, and it should have those fancy Brunswick automatic pinsetters that you wanted.

FRED [blushing, ducks his head]: Yes.

PASTOR: But I was wondering if you're aware that Milo filed an application to spend next summer in Madagascar with our medical team. Mr. Miyagi is willing to pay his way over.

FRED: Wait just a minute. Mr. Miyagi?

PASTOR: He's vice president of a big bank here in the city and his daughter Kim . . .

FRED: Oh, now I understand.

PASTOR: Well, Milo wanted me to talk to you and . . .

ERMA [returning into the room with teacups and tea]: Pastor, we're so glad you called. [Erma sets the tea before each of them as she talks.] . . . Aren't we, Fred?

FRED: You won't be, Erma, when you hear what he's going to say. Milo's going to Madagascar.

ERMA [nearly dropping her teacup]: Madagascar!

FRED: See what your missions concern has produced?

PASTOR: There's no need to be so alarmed, Fred. Milo assures me that he will not even consider it without your complete blessing on the idea.

ERMA: But how . . .

FRED: Kim's dad, the banker, wants to subsidize his trip . . . just for the summer.

PASTOR: Just for the summer and just with your permission, otherwise I know Milo will not want to go.

ERMA: Well . . . I . . . I . . . I think this is wonderful, Fred. I told you Milo was changing. Remember C. T. Studd?

FRED: I remember, Erma . . . but Milo . . . he's so young. . . .

ERMA: He is young, but he is eighteen . . . C. T. Studd was a young man too when he . . .

FRED: Cool it on Studd, Erm . . .

PASTOR: It will be doubly important that Milo feels your support after I'm gone.

ERMA: Gone!

FRED: I forgot to tell you, Erm, the pastor came to tell us he was leaving.

ERMA: Leaving! How can you? We need you! I need you. And Milo will be crushed. He's grown to think so much of you, Pastor. I'm sure you realize that for the last several months Milo has been saving his lunch money as a part of your mission to Madagascar projects.

PASTOR: Yes, I realize it, Erma. Not only that, but he has led many others to do the same. He really is a fine young man.

ERMA: But do you have to leave the church right now, I mean, this soon, Pastor?

PASTOR: The parsonage sold today. So we've made up our minds that this is the best way to handle it. By the way, Fred, I just called on Stu and Blondie earlier tonight, and they asked me to give you this and have you look it over.

FRED [taking a large envelope from the pastor and opening it]: Oh, it looks like a supplier's catalog. [Fred opens the catalog to a page marked with a clip.]

PASTOR: Stu said there were two kinds of automatic pinsetters in there and that you should select the one you like best, and he'll return the catalog to the architect.

FRED [mumbles]: All right . . .

PASTOR: Shall I tell Mr. Miyagi that you approve of Milo's going?

FRED: Well, I don't know. I'll need some time to think about it.

PASTOR: Well, take some time. We don't have to decide the whole thing tonight. I might tell you that Mr. Miyagi is as taken with Milo as we all are. He wanted me to tell you that he'll be glad to help you arrange whatever Milo needs for scholastic loans to get him in school once he's back from Madagascar at the end of summer.

FRED: If he goes.

PASTOR: Of course!

ERMA [hiding a case of the sniffles]: Fred, Pastor, I've got such mixed feelings. I'm so sorry you're leaving, Pastor. But I can't believe our little boy has so much interest in Madagascar. . . . I'm honored . . . but I'm afraid.

PASTOR: No need to be afraid. Milo isn't. Do you know what he told me the other night?

ERMA: What?

PASTOR: He told me he had been reading the biography of C. T. Studd and . . .

FRED: C. T. Studd!

PASTOR: Did I say something wrong?

ERMA: Not at all. What did Milo say?

PASTOR: He said that it is hard to imagine that God would call so many pastors to minister here in America and so few to serve him in all the rest of the world, and then he said . . .

FRED: Then he said what?

PASTOR: Maybe there are more reasons to live than Sunday afternoon football and rock concerts.

FRED: Well, maybe more than rock concerts but . . .

PASTOR: He said that he was glad he had once won a letterman's jacket in track, but there was a race he longed to run where the only runners were distance runners. Then he quoted 1 Corinthians 9:24-27. Do you know what it says?

FRED: Sure . . .

ERMA: Oh, Fred, isn't this wonderful? I wonder why Milo never told us. Maybe we never turned off the television long enough to talk about it.

PASTOR: Well, I guess I had best be going. [Pastor stands and so do Fred and Erma. He turns to walk toward the door.]

MILO [bursting in the room excitedly]: Mom, Dad, I got a job cleaning the bank at night from nine till midnight . . . Oh . . . Pastor . . . You're here? . . . I mean . . . it's good to see you.

FRED: Mr. Miyagi's bank?

MILO: Yes, Dad . . . Pastor . . . I . . . it's good to have you here. Wow! Your Bible study groups on Tuesday night are special. Kim thinks so too! What are . . . I mean, why . . . ?

ERMA: The pastor came to tell us he is leaving.

MILO: Leaving? The church? For good?

PASTOR: For good, Milo. I need your prayers that I can find another one.

MILO [biting his lip]: But there's so much more I need to learn . . .

PASTOR: You will learn, not because I am here or gone, but

because it is in your heart to learn.

MILO [in a flood of emotion embraces the pastor and the two stand interlocked for a moment]: Thanks so much for all . . . for everything!

PASTOR: Well, good-bye all. May the Lord keep you in his peace!

[Releasing Milo, he shakes hands with Fred and Erma and leaves.]

ERMA [after the door is closed]: Oh, Fred, he left without taking the bowling equipment catalog.

MILO: So that's it, Dad. Well . . . at least you'll have your automatic Brunswick pinsetters . . . [Milo turns on his heel and hurries out of the room.]

ERMA [stands silent a moment]: Oh, Fred. . . .

FRED: Where's my Bible?

ERMA: Why, Fred?

FRED: Erma, I have no idea what 1 Corinthians 9:24-27 even says.

ERMA [hurrying to coffee table, picks up a Bible]: Me either, Fred . . . shall I read it?

FRED: Of course, of course . . .

ERMA: "Know ye not that they which run in a race run all, but one receiveth the prize? So run, that ye may obtain. And every man that striveth for the mastery is temperate in all things. Now they do it to obtain a corruptible crown; but we an incorruptible. I therefore so run, not as uncertainly; so fight I, not as one that beateth the air: But I keep under my body, and bring it into subjection: lest that by any means, when I have preached to others, I myself should be a castaway."

# ACT V

# Scene I

# When Calling a Pastor, Run Faster

[It is about two months later. Fred and Erma have just entered the church business meeting and are talking together before the meeting officially begins. Stu and Blondie Johnston see Fred and Erma and call out to them.]

ERMA: Hi, Stu and Blondie.

FRED: Hi, you two. Isn't that a new frock, Blondie?

BLONDIE: Well, yes, Fred!

STU: It is? How much, Blondie?

FRED: Oops! Hope I didn't start anything! Sorry, Blondie!

BLONDIE: That's okay, Fred. Like it, Stu?

STU: How much, Blondie? Looks like Discount City wasn't good enough for you this time.

BLONDIE: Please, Stu, I need some new clothes. The Lord always wants us to look our best.

STU: Blondie, our Lord wants us to be humble and shop at Discount City. . . . How much?

BLONDIE: Sit down, Stu. [Stu complies and sits down.] Well, it was a marked-down dress. I got it for only $127.00. [Stu jumps up.]

STU: What is it made out of—the Shroud of Turin? Look, Blondie, I want you to look nice, but you can look nice shopping at Discount City. Oh, honey, I'm sorry. . . . Look, this is going to be a very special weekend. I'm glad you're going to look nice. Well, this is the Sunday we have the ground-breaking services for the Christian Life Center. We'll be turning the first shovels of dirt and presenting the bulldozer keys to the contractor. I can hardly wait till you put your pretty little sacrificial foot on that gold spade . . . then we . . .

FRED: Well, I want all our family up early this Sunday 'cause I want to be sure we can find a parking place. There's going to be a lot of people there.

STU: Blondie's invited the governor's daughter. . . . Isn't she a friend of your boy, Erma?

ERMA: Well, yes, but Milo asked to be excused for this Sunday.

FRED: Milo? He's crazy about church, Erm. Why would he want to be excused? He, above all people, should want to be in church.

ERMA: Well, he does want to be in church . . . just not ours, Fred. He wants to go to a new little church that's meeting down in the city. He thought he might be of more real help there.

FRED: Well . . . I . . . but this Sunday! How new is this church?

ERMA: He said it was only about a month old now.

FRED: Well . . . I'll be . . . I guess I can't coerce him into going to our church if he really wants to go somewhere else. If it's such a new church, how does he know it will last?

ERMA: I don't know, Fred. But he sure seems excited about it. He said Kim Miyagi and several of the other young people are going there too.

FRED: One month, huh? [suddenly, as if overtaken by insight] Erm, how long has Smith been gone?

ERMA: I think about four weeks now, hasn't he?

BLONDIE: Hey, you two! Let's grab a seat. King Sizemore is about to call this meeting to order!

KING [rising and clearing his throat]: I want to thank each of you for electing me chairman of the board while the church continues to search for a new pastor.

LUELLA COLBY: What happened to our old one, King?

KING: Well, Luella, he felt called somewhere else where he'd be truly happy in the service of the Lord.

LUELLA: Where maybe he would also have somewhere else to live, King. Is it true that you sold the parsonage out from under the man?

KING: Well, Luella, I wouldn't exactly say we sold it out from under the man. The house was old and in need of repair, and we felt that if we were ever going to sell it this would be a good time in order to dump the profits into the Christian Life Center.

LUELLA: The old place must have brought about thirty pieces of silver, huh, King?

KING: Now wait just a minute, Luella. I know you and the others on the missions committee liked the direction Pastor Smith was taking us. But the whole board made the decision. Fred, here, made the motion and . . .

LUELLA: Fred, is that true?

FRED: Well, yes, Luella . . . we all thought that . . .

LUELLA: Who's "we" Fred? You and King and Stu and Harry?

STU: Don't drag my name into this, Luella Colby. Blondie and I both have been very sacrificial. . . .

LUELLA: Yes, and the sacrificial lamb was Pastor Smith. You all have homes and cars and securities. Maybe you didn't know this, but after Pastor Smith came back from the mission field, a series of illnesses in his family kept him from ever building much of a retirement program. I wouldn't say across the years that Tranquility Community Church has been at all generous to him. And now, well . . . this had to come as the supreme blow. Just when we should have drawn around him with love and support, we've turned him out to pasture . . . and thin pasture at that.

KING: Now wait a minute, Luella, we are not turning him out to pasture. The man left of his own accord.

LUELLA: His own accord? A salary totally inadequate to find another place to live and a church that made a Judas project of a Christian Life Center so that they could have a roller rink and Brunswick automatic pinsetting machines! Yes, Stu, you and Blondie are very sacrificial people, sacrificing everything to your own needs for pre-eminence in this church. [standing] I don't know if any of you cared enough to ask what happened to Pastor Smith, but he's gone down into the city and opened up a small mission in a storefront. Some of our young people are helping him, and they have been working with some people who wouldn't be able to contribute much in this kind of congregation. I, for one, plan to join him and see if there's anything I can do to help. [Luella walks out of the meeting.]

STU: Well, good riddance! King, I suggest that we pray and seek God's leadership as we look for a new pastor. . . . I'd like to lead if I could.

KING: Certainly.

STU: Dear God, bless our church and this wonderful building program and guide us as we look for a new pastor, one that is truly after your heart. And, God, may we find such a man as will see this entire city with all of its needs. Help all of those people in our congregation who are made to see our sense of humility and sacrifice to try to become more like Christ and ourselves. Amen.

KING: Amen. Now do we have any suggestions about the way to

look for a new pastor?

HARRY: Well, King, why don't you appoint a search committee and have them call Roller Institute of the Prophets. A church that my uncle goes to got a RIP graduate, and they had over seven hundred additions in the first three years he was there. You know, King, since we are getting this new Christian Life Center, we ought to look for a younger man who's a little more athletically inclined. . . . Don't you think so, Fred?

FRED: I guess so, Stu. . . .

HARRY: Well, if you ask me, we for sure don't need an older man who's always preaching on evangelizing the world and feeding its hungry or trying to get the church to get concerned about people we don't even know. We have got to be more concerned about our needs here . . . course, his wife should play the piano or organ, but mostly he should be a little more athletic.

KING: What about his faith? He should be positive and believe in a blood-bought Scripture memory program . . .

MADGE: . . . and sing the old hymns.

BLONDIE: . . . and hate rock and roll. Don't forget that.

KING: Well, if we get someone from Gil Roller's institute, they hate rock and roll. They hate nearly everything out there, don't you think? I mean, sin, mostly. Fred, you're being awfully quiet tonight.

FRED: Yes, King. I've been doing a lot of thinking. My Milo is one of the young people who has gone into the city with Pastor Smith, and I'm having a lot of second thoughts about whether or not any of us has done the right thing.

KING: You know what Roller says in *The View from the Top:* "Successful men are not always right, but they are never in doubt!" Fred, I'm surprised to hear you say we were wrong.

FRED: Well, I don't mean altogether wrong, but maybe we didn't think through everything like we should have. I was too blind to see that Pastor Smith was influencing Milo in a direction that was important to Milo. I was a fool not to see it earlier.

BLONDIE: Well, I hope that you're not implying that Stu and I were wrong. We gave every last cent of our inheritance to show the world how much we love the Lord. . . . How can you say we were wrong? [begins crying]

FRED: Now, Blondie, I admire what you did, and I know you did it for the right reasons, but . . .

KING: Well, now . . . I think we just need to carry all this to the Lord in prayer and get that committee forged to write the Roller Institute of the Prophets. I'm sure we'll be getting a new pastor that will help each of us as we set new vistas of achievement. Do you agree, Fred?

FRED: Yes, O King! . . . er . . . I mean, oh yes, King!

# S c e n e  II

# Daddy Sings the Blues

[Fred is trying to watch the basketball playoffs and is so absorbed that he hears little else that is going on around him. Milo is talking on the phone to Kim. Dawn Marie is sometimes coloring in a *Bible Children of the World* coloring book and sometimes humming and sometimes practicing for her ballet recital.]

DAWN MARIE: Daddy, what color are faces? I gotta color the faces now!

FRED [still watching television]: Brown . . . Why is he trying that play from that far out? He needs to work the ball!

DAWN MARIE: I want these to be like Madagascar people, Daddy! Light brown or dark brown?

FRED: Wait till the commercial, Dawn Marie. What's the matter with the ref? He's blind!!

DAWN MARIE [laying down her coloring book]: Daddy, you wanna see what I learned at ballet? Hop . . . hop . . . hop!

FRED [not listening]: Don't hop till the commercial, Dawn Marie. Throw it . . . throw the ball, stupid . . . look, Murdock is open . . . he's wide-open . . . give him the ball, you idiot! [Fred kicks the coffee table.] He must have learned basketball from a croquet instructor. What a dope!

DAWN MARIE: Hop . . . hop . . . spin and pirouette. Daddy, if you can hum "Bess, You Is My Woman," I can show you how I do my leap and pass and end in the splits . . . hop . . . hop . . . hop.

FRED: Well, it's about time they pulled him out of the game! Rookie loser! Murdock's fine but he can't sink those baskets without help. Those guys must be blind.

DAWN MARIE: Hop . . . Hummmmmmmmmmmmmm . . . Daddy, do you know the end part of "Bess, You Is My Woman"?

[Fred reaches forward and turns up the television.]

MILO: Dad, please, I'm talking to Kim. *Excuse me, Kim, Dad's got the TV turned up* . . . Oh, it's no use. [Milo says good-bye and hangs up.]

DAWN MARIE [singing louder, still dancing]: *Hop . . . hop . . . glide . . . glide . . . Daddy . . . are you sure you don't know the last part of "Bess, You Is My Woman"? Hop . . . hop . . . hop! See, Daddy, see, here's my passing glide . . . Daddy . . . you want me to put on my toe shoes?*

FRED: Dawn Marie, will you please go back to your room and color?

DAWN MARIE: But Daddy, light brown or dark brown?

FRED [at last turning down the TV]: Well, the first quarter is over. [turning to Dawn Marie] Now what's the problem? [Dawn Marie starts crying.] Oh, for heaven's sake, what's the matter?

MILO: She wants you to tell her if people's faces are dark brown or light brown in Madagascar.

FRED: Is that all?

MILO: No, she also wants you to hum the last part of "Bess, You Is My Woman"!

FRED: I never heard of it!

MILO: It's George Gershwin. It's from *Porgy and Bess.*

FRED: George Schwinn, the bicyclemaker? Wrote songs? [Dawn Marie still crying] Ah, Dawn Marie, don't cry . . . faces are light brown, Dawn Marie. Now stop crying and start coloring . . . Oh, oh, second quarter! Go practice your splits in your room. Daddy wants to see them later.

MILO: Daddy can hardly wait, Dawn Marie. Daddy wants to see your splits later . . . much later . . . right after the playoffs and before football season starts.

FRED: That's better, Murdock . . . good show. [Fred turns up the TV and moves in.] Look . . . you lanky dummy, throw the ball to Murdock, the murderer. [Fred slams his coffee cup on the table, obviously angry.] Look, you dope! *If you can't throw the ball get out of the way.*

MILO: Dad, Wall Street is collapsing. We're in a national economic emergency.

FRED: *Murdock . . . it's your third foul and it's only the second quarter! It's okay to knock those boys on the floor, but do it when the ref's not looking.*

MILO: Dad, we're under massive nuclear attack. It's the end of the world. I'm taking the Cheerios and going to the basement.

FRED: Hah . . . he missed the free throw. . . . *He missed the cotton-pickin' free throw right on national television.* I hope to heaven his mother was watching from her wheelchair.

DAWN MARIE: Hop . . . hop. [having quit crying, is singing] Bess, you is my woman . . . [Dawn Marie hops out and Milo retreats to his room.]

ERMA [entering with a cup of coffee]: Hi, coach!

FRED: Murdock. Bench him! Coach, get him off that court! He's been on marijuana the entire weekend. *I wanna remind you guys that you can be sold to a farm club in Dubuque!*

ERMA: Fred . . . *Fred* . . . FRED!

FRED: Wait till a time-out, Erm.

ERMA [walking over and turning off the set]: Fred, there's something you ought to know.

FRED: What the . . . Can't it wait, Erm?

ERMA: No, it can't wait, and you can't hide from life any longer with your nose stuck in a television tube . . . Fred, both of your children are in their rooms.

FRED: That's good. It must mean I'm a good father.

ERMA: They're in their rooms precisely because you're not a good father. Dawn Marie needs some of your time and Milo's going to be leaving for Madagascar on Thursday. I think he'd like to see just a little of you before he goes.

FRED: Erma . . . I . . . I'm confused. It seems like our whole world is falling apart right now with Milo leaving and Dawn Marie growing up so fast. King Sizemore told me that if you train up a child in the way that he should go when he is old he will not depart from it. It's from Proverbs, I think. Well, I must have been doing something right. Milo is so religious he is going to die poor eating monkeys in Madagascar, and Dawn Marie . . . well, she's too little to tell.

ERMA: While she is little, Fred, spend some time with her so that when she's big she'll remember that you did and so will you, and you won't have any lingering regrets about the years you lost on television!

FRED: Okay, Erm, I'll tell you what. Since Milo only has two more nights at home, I'll take you all to the ice cream parlor.

ERMA: When, Fred?

FRED: Right now, Erma.

ERMA: Great. Hey, kids . . . Milo, Dawn Marie! [Phone rings.]

FRED: I'll get it, Erma. You get the kids to the car. [Erma exits. Fred lifts the receiver.] Hello . . . King . . . well, yes I do have something important going on right now. . . . Well, no, I'm not watching the playoffs right at the moment . . . but . . . I don't think so. . . . No, King, I'm going to take my children to the ice cream parlor. . . . I'll meet you later in the week, but not now. Okay? . . . Then on Saturday night . . . the whole committee! This must be something pretty big! Sure. Yes. Good-bye, King.

DAWN MARIE [bursting in the room]: Daddy, is it true you're turning off the TV just to take us to the ice cream parlor?

FRED: Well, not just to take you to the ice cream parlor, Dawn Marie. Before we go, I for one would like to see your rendition of "Bess, You Is My Woman"! [Erma and Milo enter.] I've always loved George Schwinn, even when he used to make bicycles.

ERMA [cupping her hand]: It's George Gershwin, Fred.

MILO: Dad, I'm sorry what I said about that nuclear war.

FRED: What nuclear war, son? Tomorrow night I want to take all of us out for a nice dinner before we send you off for the summer.

MILO: Gosh, Dad, you're the best. . . . Here, Dawn Marie, I'll put the Gershwin tape in the cassette player and you can show us your stuff!

# Scene III

# Going Home

[The scene is a small storefront chapel which will hold only a few dozen people, but it is full. Pastor Smith is standing up to speak.]

PASTOR: My text this morning is taken from Mark 6:1-6. In this passage Jesus is going home. Remember home? That wonderful retreat three quiet blocks off any main street—we all look forward to going home, don't we? Jesus did too. Home for him was an ideal shrine—a shelter from the storm that was gathering all about him.

How and where is your home? Can you call up its image? That soft chair to rest in at night. That special haven where your hurried life slows to a walk.

Home is never tired. It cannot know fatigue. Rest—real Matthew 11:28 rest—waits in that grand house of a thousand memories. Your busy schedule dies—burns its unimportant agenda and sets you free.

There is always excitement about going home. Once in that retreat, warm peace strips away the grime of work.

In Mark 6:1 Jesus comes home. He has only ministered for a year, but it has been a furious year, and he is ready for a rest. The lines of people waiting to be healed have stretched out before him night and day. Crowds have mobbed him. His enemies have badgered him as he tried to teach his beloved Twelve.

Tired? Jesus tired? Yes, the man-God Jesus is so much man, he is worn out with life. But now he is going home. Home to the carpenter shop of his father where he played hide and seek behind the old workbench! Home to the clay hearth where his mother baked steaming barley loaves and roast kid! Home where his younger brothers and sisters would still want to do carefree things and play children's games. Home where Jude and James and Joseph, Jr., would share in wine and laughter. Above all, home—blessed rest!

Of course at home there would be all the neighbors who had watched him grow up. There would be the grand old ladies of Nazareth who had nursed him through fevers with their homemade remedies, the farmers for whom Jesus' skilled hands had fastened ox yokes. He and they would live again! Oh, the conversations he would have at the city well! Home . . . home . . . home!

Jesus had left the town over a year before to seek John the Baptist. Shortly after his baptism he went alone into the wilderness for six weeks. Down the alkaline canyons of the Dead Sea and through the thick jungles of the Jordan, Jesus celebrated God's will and came out of the desert as a man with a mission. He preached in the fields, drawing even greater crowds than John the Baptist. He preached in little amphitheaters carved by nature and the Galilean Sea. His reputation and schedule grew as one. He had become the most talked-about man in all Palestine—the celebrity of Nazareth—that dusty little one-camel hamlet of dried adobe houses!

Because he had become so well known, he was asked to preach in the synagogue he had once attended. The people of Nazareth were both impressed and depressed by the sermon that they heard that first Sabbath that Jesus was back.

Home listened and debated his return and himself! "Is not this the carpenter, the son of Mary, the brother of James, and Joses, and of Juda, and Simon? and are not his sisters here with us? And they were offended at him." Now he, their not-so-heroic home-town hero, must hear the sneer in that word *carpenter*. Well has it been said that familiarity breeds contempt! The hometown is the arena where our security crumbles all too quickly: our rest gets swallowed up in the criticism of those who know us too well.

Home, the harsh haven where we fit into the schedule and demands of those who know exactly where everybody else fits. Jesus a hero! Nonsense! What right does he have to heroism? Isn't this Mary's boy who goes around talking to himself and mumbling in distant cities that he is more than he has the right to be? They are shocked by his unpredictable self-defense and gross fantasy. Jesus, Lord of heaven? This is too great a claim. Lover of the whole world at once? We cannot contain it.

"Nazareth!" bellows Nathanael in John 1, "Can there any good thing come out of Nazareth?" Nathanael had seen the little sun-baked adobe village and could see no possibility of a Messiah coming from a place so unimpressive.

"The Son of God? Never!" they cried. "Nothing but the son of Mary and Joseph. You grew up with our children. We toddled you as a child; taught you in the synagogue. You cannot be God's Son!"

His childhood seemed too small to support such cosmic

claims. They knew Jesus too well to see him in any larger light.

Our church is brand-new! What would God wish for us most of all? He would want a membership that *knew* Jesus and not just knew about Jesus. That is what went wrong with the people in Jesus' hometown. They were not irreligious. They were deeply religious. They had a synagogue. They sang the psalms in their services. They burned the candles and taught tithing. They had a robed rabbi and cantor. But as Jesus closed his sermon in Nazareth, he reminded the villagers that God's love was as wide as the world itself. They grew angry at his suggestion that they were no more special in his love than Gentiles. We must make sure we don't see ourselves as the only special objects of God's love. When we do, we grow blind to our world obligation. In Nazareth their exclusiveness led to a riot. In our churches it dwindles into apathy.

Life went on in Nazareth but Jesus left never to return. He remained for them only the son of Mary and never the Son of God. He was Jesus unappealing because he talked too globally about God's love. How was life afterward in Nazareth? We can only guess! What happens when Christ's great sovereignty is reduced to make him only the special Lord of the select and lucky few? Egotism rises, servanthood gives up the towel and basin. Men quarrel over chief seats.

We are too Nazarene—captured by little religious routines, loving in little ways, turned inward so our ears hear only that which amuses or affirms us. Our eyes cannot see beyond our gaudy parade. Pity us, Father-God. There are still bleak, arid landscapes, destroyed by human hatred.

There is only one answer to those of us who think we know Jesus. We must widen our world as we examine our own unworthy lives. Then our ears will hear the silent crying of all men, and our eyes will see even the most distant invisible hurts. And we shall enter full at last into his presence and acclaim him Lord of the whole world at once because he is our joy, our very way of life. Amen. So be it.

I would like to conclude this morning's service by introducing to you Mr. Fred Miyagi.

FRED [whispering to Erma]: I didn't know his name was Fred too. I can't believe he would go to such a simple church!

MR. MIYAGI: Pastor Smith was kind enough to let me say a few words to you this morning. I have been as guilty as anyone of knowing about Jesus without bowing before him. My daughter Kim is with the Madagascar mission this summer. She was the one who taught me that Christ can't be known through our prestigious positions or complex church machinery. I've come in simple faith to call him Lord. I only did this a few weeks ago. Since that time, I've found that Christ is only Lord to those who call him Lord and God, to those who seek him from a hungry soul that only Christ can satisfy.

PASTOR: Thank you.

ERMA: Fred, I've got to get up there . . . I . . . [Erma rises.]

FRED: Sit down, Erma. What are you doing?

ERMA: Excuse me, Pastor Smith. May I say a few words?

PASTOR: Certainly, Erma. Friends, this is Erma MacArthur.

ERMA: I, like Mr. Miyagi, have just come to understand the Christ I knew so much about yet never knew at all. I have wronged this fine pastor. . . .

PASTOR: How have you wronged me, Erma?

ERMA: By not speaking out when others misjudged you. The great sins are the frequent ones. The frequent ones are made by those who may not offer evil judgments but sit quietly while others do. Pastor, I ask your forgiveness.

PASTOR: It's not necessary, Erma. I never felt your judgment, and I know your faith to be the finest . . . still . . . we all have inner needs. We are all one in the love of the best Forgiver . . . So let us stand and say our benediction.

ALL: Christ is the Lord of all our doubt.
He fills our desolation.
Sing of his renewing joy,
And seek his consecration.

# S c e n e  IV

# A Letter
# from Milo

[Dawn Marie is playing with dolls. Erma and Fred are reading. The phone rings. Fred answers.]

FRED: King . . . oh, hello. . . . No, I don't think I care much about the equipment for Tranquility Community. You're having an RIP candidate this weekend? . . . No, I guess we won't be there. . . . I don't know if we'll ever be there again or not . . . thanks for calling. [hangs up]

ERMA: You like the mission church downtown?

FRED: Yeah, Erm . . . Hey, how about if all three of us go out for dinner tonight. I think Dawn Marie really misses Milo. Do you know what 2 Corinthians 5:17 says?

ERMA: Something about the Bushwackers?

FRED: Don't mock me, Erma. It says, "If any man be in Christ, he is a new creature." Remember, it was the text of the pastor's sermon on Sunday.

ERMA: Fred, what's happened to you? I can't remember a time when we ever talked about the pastor's sermon in the middle of the week.

FRED: Well, I've made up my mind. I'm going to be a new man this year. Further, I am going to become a kinder man with a soft and gentle spirit.

ERMA: Fred, are you well?

FRED: And I've been praying more and reading the Bible every day . . . Erma, I want to ask you to forgive me for not being the support I should have been to you these past years. And Erm, I love you! Those are three little words that you are going to be hearing a lot of from now on.

DAWN MARIE: Wow! Daddy, this is great! Are you also going to quit hollering on the freeway?

ERMA: Now, Dawn Marie, don't expect too much. Daddy's only human.

FRED: Erma, I'm ashamed for all the times that I haven't been what you've needed in your spiritual life.

ERMA: Dawn Marie, where are you going?

DAWN MARIE: To get my little red tape recorder.

FRED: And Dawn Marie, I'm going to every piano recital; I just love to hear you play . . . and after supper, every Thursday, I'm going to play dolls with you for thirty minutes.

DAWN MARIE: Daddy, could I have a dollar a week allowance?

FRED: Dawn Marie, when I was your age I got twenty-five cents a week! Money . . . money, *money! Dawn Marie, do you think I'm made of the stuff?*

ERMA: Fred, do you have to shout?

FRED: *Erma, Dawn Marie must think I'm one of the Vanderbilts . . . one dollar a week. . . . Do you realize that's fifty-two dollars a year, Dawn Marie? Out of the question!*

DAWN MARIE: Daddy, remember 2 Corinthians 5:17. When we finish playing on Thursday night, you won't break my Barbie dolls and holler at me, will you?

FRED [simmering down]: Okay, look honey, I'm sorry. One dollar a week!

DAWN MARIE: Daddy, would you buy me a new sports car for my dolls? It only costs seventeen dollars. . . . Remember 2 Corinthians 5:17.

FRED: Erm, why do people always take advantage of a truly spiritual man? Why are spiritual resolutions the hardest to live up to?

ERMA: They're not unless we try to do them in our own strength. Fred, excuse me. I'm going out to get the mail before we leave. Could be a letter from . . . [runs out of the room]

FRED: Erm, I've got a lot to learn. It's time to go, Dawn Marie.

[Erma returns waving an envelope.]

DAWN MARIE: Milo!

FRED: Well, don't just stand there, Erm, read it . . . out loud too!

ERMA [eagerly tears it open and reads]: "Dear Mom and Dad, I've met some wonderful people since I've been here. There is a surgeon who has worked out here for thirty-five years. The people all really love him and need him."

FRED: I'm sure all that monkey meat must upset their systems after a few years.

ERMA [continues reading]: "Well, Dad, they don't eat monkey meat at all. They live in houses and while they are not quite as nice as ours, they are always clean and very pretty."

FRED: Still, I'll bet they have a difficult time getting to them without roads.

ERMA [continues]: "The roads here are just terrific! Two of the missionaries have motorcycles that we use to visit the little towns that are farthest away . . ." Oh, Fred, Milo knows how I feel about motorcycles. I do so hope he wears a helmet.

FRED: Now, Erma, don't get upset.

ERMA [continuing to read]: "Mom, I know how you feel about motorcycles so I am always careful to wear my helmet every time I get on one of them. The roads are pretty congested, and I can't really go all that fast anyway.

"One of the great things I am discovering is that God is still alive doing wonderful things in the lives of all who will trust him and let him work. I have memorized Joshua 1:9, 'Have not I commanded thee? Be strong and of a good courage; be not afraid, neither be thou dismayed: for the LORD thy God is with thee withersoever thou goest.' It suddenly occurred to me that it doesn't matter how far or how long our separation is. God will never leave us. Isn't that a great promise?"

FRED: I can't believe that this is the same old Milo! He sure has changed. It sounds like he is going to turn out to be a preacher someday.

ERMA [continuing to read]: "I can't believe all the changes that have come about in my life. I'm sure it must sound like I'm going to be a preacher someday. Well, I wouldn't know about that. I sure do admire this surgeon. Whenever I see his hands touching these people to heal them, I am made to think of the hands of Christ. Then I want to be like Christ, and then at other times I want to be like the surgeon. Although I suspect that to be like the one would be to be very like the other.

"How is Dad coming along on the church board? Is the Christian Life Center under way? I can just see Dad with those new Brunswick automatic pinsetters. He loves those things like these people love God."

FRED: Wow! Erma, that seems so harsh to me.

ERMA [continues reading]: "Anyway, when Dad gets the chance to use them I know he'll be glad that the church has them.

"Unfortunately, it will be a long time over here till they have Brunswick bowling equipment right in the church. But they have some other wonderful things that are harder to find in American churches. They have things like a hunger to know God and talk to him. While they don't seem to have a lot of this world's goods, they are utterly generous. I can't brag about anything they have in their homes or they will just give it to me."

DAWN MARIE: Mommy, did he ask about me in the letter?

FRED: Shh, Dawn Marie, and listen.

DAWN MARIE: I am listening, but I've written him three letters and I wish he would ask about me.

ERMA [continues]: "How is Dawn Marie? Tell her to write me and let me know how things are going in church and how she is enjoying film night this summer. Tell her it's okay if she reads my letters by the exit light!"

DAWN MARIE: Mommy, how come he tells me to write when I have already written three letters?

FRED: Well, mail goes to Madagascar by camel and . . .

ERMA: Now, Fred. Well, Dawn Marie, it does take a long time for mail to get there. I'm sure Milo will be getting your letters very soon now. [continues reading] "I remember you in my prayers and trust you will do the same. Kim sends her love as well. I'm going with the doctor to one of the smaller villages this afternoon. May God watch over all of us till we are together."

FRED [choked with emotion]: Erma, there's something special about that kid.

ERMA: Why, Fred, you're crying. . . . What's the matter?

FRED: Oh, nothing, Erma. I just wish I'd let him have the car a little more than I did.

DAWN MARIE: That was a nice letter, wasn't it, Daddy? Well, Daddy, it's Thursday night and you know what 2 Corinthians 5:17 says.

FRED: I know, honey. After dinner, it's the dolls.

# S c e n e V

# A Letter from Dad

MILO [sitting under a palm tree]: Hey, Kim, something happened to Dad.

KIM: What do you mean?

MILO: Listen to this letter I just got. [reading] "Dear Son, I feel so foolish in so many ways. I met Mr. Miyagi at church and we went out to lunch afterward. He is a wonderful man. He had a hamburger and French fries, and I don't think it was just because they don't serve raw fish, either.

"I wanted to tell you that, while I've got a long ways to go, I want to be more like the surgeon you talked about in your last letter. I've been going to the little mission regularly now, and I'm finding that when a church has a lot of heart in it you can get by without automatic pinsetters and not even miss them.

"I want to help you in any way I can as you enroll in college. I don't care anymore if you won't be rich and influential . . . well, maybe a little rich wouldn't hurt. But above all, I want you to be all that you think God would want you to be. I'm not much of a letter writer, so I'll close for now. Be careful if you try to get your own anaconda skin. My regards to Kim. Love, Dad."

KIM: Hey, our parents are getting to be friends. That's great.

MILO: You bet, Kim. My dad is changing a lot.

KIM: Mine too.

MILO: Well, it's time for lunch. Wanna walk with me to the dining compound?

KIM: Sure. Milo, did you ever tell your dad that we haven't had a bite of monkey since we've been here?

MILO: Yes, but he convinces very slowly, Kim! Kim, are you going to State U when our tour is over this summer?

KIM: I guess so. I'm pre-enrolled there this spring. I want to do something with my life like these missionaries are doing. I want to be able to say that I used my life in the best possible way.

MILO: Me too. What's for lunch?

KIM: Let's see, this is Thursday. Fried fish, fresh vegetables and iced tea, isn't it?

MILO: I think you're right. Well, let's go eat.

KIM: Okay.

MILO [as they begin walking off]: Kim, would you have any time after lunch to help me wrestle an anaconda?

KIM: Not a chance, Milo. For that kind of activity you need the good, solid nutrition of monkey sandwiches.

# Postlude

MILO: Excuse me. . . . The play's over. . . . If you want your money back you'll have to work that out with the management. Right now I've got to start packing to get back to America. I just cashed my stipend from the mission board and spent it all on shoes. I'm going to deliver them to the kids in the village. I won't have any money to take home, but there's a lot of hookworm out in the villages and there's a simple cure—shoes. Besides, I get a kick out of this. I can buy these shoes for pennies—they're factory seconds, though it doesn't matter much to these kids. It's all such great work! It makes me feel real somehow.

I'm a little reluctant to go home. Not that life has been easy here. The mosquitoes are troublesome. The heat is sometimes stifling. Most of all I've discovered Madagascar has its share of small-minded people. I even met a man in one of the churches who thinks people in Madagascar should not give money to world missions till they have built nicer church buildings here. He didn't mention bowling centers; still, he seemed a lot like Harry and Stu and King. So values and virtues are scrambled in every part of the world.

Still, my life hasn't been the same since I came here. The well-dressed Christians I knew back home never seemed to have the joy I often see in this part of the world. I will never forget the radiant faces of these dark men and women singing a vespers hymn.

I wonder how Pastor Smith is doing in his new church. No bowling there! It's okay! I never liked bowling much anyway. I guess it's the explosive sound of that heavy ball hitting those weak and wobbly, unsteady pins, smashing and scattering the flying wood. There's a lot of brutality in this world, I'm afraid.

I don't know how to answer much of it. Sometimes I feel I've been too much the pin in life and too little the ball. But most of the time I feel good about serving Christ. Back home I never knew there was this world of hurt and need.

At Tranquility Community Church they have a new pastor who is everything Stu and Blondie ever wanted. I'm sure he preaches just the way Gil Roller does and he, no doubt, has King Sizemore memorizing all the Scripture he can between bowling nights.

Well, I better get moving. This is no plea for funds. Still, if ever you have anything to spare at the end of the month, we could use a little money in the Madagascar Shoe Fund!

Have you ever noticed a kid with a new pair of shoes? They show them to everybody . . . specially down in the village. [stops, smiles, walks nearly offstage, stops and adds as an afterthought] Jesus once said, "Suffer the little children to come unto me . . ." Six kids out here will be able to come to him in new shoes. It's a little gift, but grace is tasty even when it's bite-sized. To hold a little in the heart and savor it is to know both life and God and to appreciate them both. I still don't know where I'm going in life [stops and pats the shoe boxes], but I think I've found a place to start. [exits]